Death of a Fading Beauty

By the same author

Blind Hate
The Destroying of Harry Blyne
Hatchet Man
The Millennium Trail
Seasnake
Death of a Dusty Lady
Death of a Lonely Warrior

Death of a Fading Beauty

Peter Moir Fotheringham

ROBERT HALE · LONDON

First published in Great Britain 2000

ISBN 0 7090 6753 4

Robert Hale Limited
Clerkenwell House
Clerkenwell Green
London EC1R 0HT

2 4 6 8 10 9 7 5 3 1

Typeset by
Derek Doyle & Associates, Liverpool.
Printed in Great Britain by
St Edmundsbury Press, Bury St Edmunds, Suffolk.
Bound by Woolnough Bookbinders Ltd

This one is for Pel and Geoff, who think Orkney is invisible

1

Called from a warm bed to a cold body. A nice way to spend a Sunday morning.

Smellie drove along Shore Road, running the electric shaver over his face as he went, spotting the flashing blue lights in the distance at the entrance to the ferry terminal. Just this once there hadn't been a clean shirt ready for him at Jane Grey's flat and he had been forced to wear yesterday's, which he hated, and there had been no time for a shower.

Whose body? Naismith had been laconic, as usual. All would be revealed soon enough.

And no breakfast. He and Jane had planned a long lie in with bacon and eggs and sausages and toast and coffee and the Sunday paper and the crossword and then, no doubt, proximity would have led to intimacy and later they would have driven the thirty miles to Brickhill, the county town, to see one of the new movies, followed by a meal and then back home for more intimacy and trying to finish off the last few awkward clues in the crossword, not necessarily in that order. He had been looking forward all week to another self-indulgent Sunday.

But now he was driving through a raw drizzle beside a grey North Sea on a November Sunday morning in answer to a call from Detective Sergeant James. . . . Correction. Detective

Inspector James Naismith. And he was now Detective Superintendent William Smellie, head of Garrmouth Division CID. Which meant a lot more responsibility and a bit more authority and a nice hike in salary but sadly did not mean he could stay in bed with Jane on a wet Sunday morning.

A uniformed officer recognized the Mazda and waved him through. Smellie drove into the ferry complex and Naismith approached and waited for him to climb out of the car. Several of the squad were standing around, shoulders hunched, collars turned up, coats and jackets and hats already wet with rain.

Promotion had not prompted Naismith to invest in new clothes to match his new status; he still looked like a man planning a day ferreting on the moors.

'Morning, sir.'

'Morning, Inspector. What do we have?'

'One dead prostitute, sir. Strangled with a length of blue polypropylene rope.'

Their eyes met. They had been working together for twelve years and understood each other very well. And they both read the daily updates from HQ in Brickhill.

'That's ominous,' Smellie said. 'Do you have an identity?'

'Sandra Sim. I know her from way back.'

'Let's have a look.'

The cluster of temporary wooden buildings had been standing against one wall of the big brick ferry terminal for many years. Yellow and black tape had been strung round the perimeter. Naismith led the way, ducking under the tape and holding it up for Smellie to follow. Drips of cold water managed to find the gap between Smellie's tweed hat and the collar of his waxed cotton coat and he shivered involuntarily.

'Probably her favourite spot,' Naismith said. 'Out of the wind, shelter from the rain.'

They edged down the narrow gap between two buildings and

turned a corner into an area about four feet wide by ten feet long, protected by an overhanging roof, wooden walls on all sides. The body lay on its face on the dirty cobbles, the short black leather skirt pushed up past the waist to reveal black stockings and bare white buttocks. Smellie saw a black leather jacket and a black plastic shoulder bag and one foot still wearing a red high-heeled shoe. The other shoe lay against the side of one of the huts. There was a length of blue polypropylene rope around the neck, partly obscured by the tangle of wet black hair.

'Who found the body, Jimmy?' They were out of earshot of the others and could forget the formalities.

'Walter Lapsley. That's his office window on the right, there. He's something to do with provisioning the ferries. He arrived for work at half past seven this morning and looked out his window at about eight o'clock and spotted the body and phoned in.'

'Check him out. Who's been here?'

'A patrol car first. They decided she was dead and called in. I've had a look at her and agree with the diagnosis. I've called Henry Jennings; he should have been here by now.'

They heard voices and looked back. Henry Jennings, the local police surgeon, came down the gap between the buildings carrying his bag. The heavy jersey and sailing jacket were a change from his usual immaculate suit.

'Morning, chaps. Congratulations on your promotions. Richly undeserved, if you ask me, but there you go. What do we have?'

'Morning, Henry.' Smellie stepped aside. 'All yours. First confirm she's dead, please, so we can get started.'

Henry looked at the white buttocks. 'That's handy. No problem about where to put the thermometer.'

He crouched over the body and used a torch and stethoscope and hands.

'Dead, all right. Probably all night, but don't use that. Details to follow.'

Smellie looked at Naismith and pulled out his mobile. 'Right, Jimmy, the usual routine. You call Parsonage and Fowler and I'll do Robbie Larch and Scene of Crime.'

While Naismith spoke to Superintendent Raymond Parsonage, the senior officer of Garrmouth. Division, Smellie called the duty officer at Police HQ in Brickhill. The message would be passed to Detective Superintendent Larch and he would call back.

Naismith was still listening to Chief Detective Inspector Norman Fowler with a bored look on his face when Smellie's mobile rang.

'Larch here, Bill. What's happening?'

'We have a dead prostitute on the docks in Garrmouth. She appears to have been strangled with a length of blue polypropylene rope.'

'Christ!'

'Thought you'd be interested.'

'What have you done?'

'We just found her,' Smellie said. 'The doc's here now; the brass have been informed; Fowler will notify the Chief Constable. I was just about to phone Scene of Crime.'

'I'll call them. I want the people who worked on the previous case. OK, Bill, I'm going to have to intrude on your territory. Leave as much as you can to me. Don't move the body.'

'Understood.'

'Where do I find you?'

'The ferry terminal. Follow the road along the shore and watch for the blue lights. It's less than half a mile from Divisional HQ.'

'In that case we'll skip the mobile incident room. I hate that bloody caravan. You have an incident room, haven't you?'

'It'll be ready shortly.'

'Right.' Larch closed the connection.

Naismith rammed his mobile into his pocket and glowered at Smellie.

'Now I know why you never speak to Fowler unless you really have to.'

'Let me guess,' Smellie said. 'Detective Superintendent Larch is on this case so we mustn't waste money by duplicating effort. Something like that?'

'On the button. Is he permanently in a bad mood as well as being obsessed with the budget?'

'Yes. But you can screw what you want out of him by feeding him a big lunch with wine. Lots of wine. Remember that; it's a useful tip. He's very keen on large puddings with custard. On the whole, though, it's better just to ignore him.'

'What's happening?'

'Robbie Larch is on his way. He'll take over.'

'So we have a serial killer?'

'That's the way it looks, Jimmy. Either that or strangling prostitutes with blue polypropylene rope is becoming a popular pastime in this county.'

Naismith stared morosely at the body.

'So what would you do in this situation, Bill? No, don't answer that. I'm supposed to know.'

He edged down the gap to the fluttering tape and Smellie smiled as he listened to his former sergeant issuing orders.

'Winston, call Inspector Noonan at home and tell her we have a murder and we'll need an incident room immediately and all available officers on duty. And I want a canteen van here as soon as possible. The van takes priority. And tell Inspector Noonan, all leave and off-duty cancelled. And tell her to notify the coroner we have a murder and we'll need a post-mortem soonest.'

Smellie watched Henry Jennings until Naismith came back.

'OK, Bill?'

'You're getting the hang of it, Jimmy. You're a natural.'

'I had a good teacher,' Naismith said modestly.

'That's odd,' Jennings said.

'What?'

'There's a pound coin here, and I'll swear it dropped out of her mouth.'

'Well spotted, Henry,' Smellie said. 'But that little snippet of information is secret. Let's keep it that way for the moment. Leave it for Scene of Crime.'

Jennings accepted the instruction without comment. He worked for a while longer then rose and brushed his knees. 'I'm finished here. The figures suggest she died about nine and a half hours ago, but I don't know how cold it got during the night so you'll have to make a generous allowance each side of that time. If by any chance I've managed to get it dead right, then she died about eleven twenty yesterday evening.'

'Thanks, Henry.'

'See you at the post-mortem.'

'You may not have to do it,' Smellie said. 'This appears to be exactly the same as a previous case, so whoever did the first post-mortem will probably be asked to do this one. Right, Jimmy, do we know a next of kin?'

They sat in Naismith's car and sipped coffee from polystyrene cups and ate rolls filled with thick slices of burnt sausage. Even with plenty of mustard there was no flavour in the food. The windows were already steaming up.

'This is not what I'd planned for breakfast,' Smellie said.

'Me neither,' Naismith mumbled, eating with appetite. 'What was that bit about the pound coin? Did the other woman have a coin in her mouth?'

'Yes. Karen Potter, prostitute, strangled with a length of blue polypropylene rope four weeks ago less than half a mile from

Police HQ. No panties found, a pound coin in her mouth. These details were not released in case they came in handy at a later stage; copycat killing, a loony confessing, a hoax call, you know how it works.'

Naismith nodded. 'So we have a travelling murderer. The last case was on a Saturday night as well. I hope we're not looking at another Yorkshire Ripper. That one wrecked a few careers.'

'They got bogged down in the mass of information they'd collected,' Smellie said. 'And they were misled by a hoax tape of someone with a Geordie accent. But they also made mistakes.'

A shadow appeared through the condensation and they heard a tapping at the driver's window. DS Grossmith and DC Winston had returned. Smellie and Naismith got out of the car.

'We found Arnold Sim, sir,' Grossmith reported. 'Husband of the dead woman. Lives just along the road a bit. Broke the news and told him he'd have to identify his wife. He'll need time to get dressed and find someone to look after the kid, then we'll collect him and take him to the hospital.'

'How did he take the news?' Smellie asked.

'Like he'd been waiting to hear it for a long time, sir. Like it was no great surprise. Like there wasn't much stuffing left in him to be knocked out.'

'It could be some time before the body's moved,' Naismith said. 'Stay with him, give him a hand, maybe take him to the canteen. I'll call you when it's time for him to go to the hospital. When he's identified her, take him to the station and get a statement. I know he's a sleazy little toerag, but handle him gently. Did you get a photograph?'

'Yes, sir. Not a great shot, but it should do. She's the one on the left.'

Smellie and Naismith studied the colour snap of three women in a pub or at some kind of function. Sandra Sim was revealed as an attractive woman with dark hair framing a narrow face.

'Get that back to the station for enlarging and copying.' Smellie called the switchboard and asked for Sarah Noonan.

'Just about set-up, sir. I've been sending people along as they arrive here.'

'Fine. Whoever comes in next can help you there. I'm sending someone along with a photograph of the dead woman: you know what to do.'

Smellie closed the connection then threw the half-eaten roll over the edge of the quay into the water. Seagulls squawked and dived.

'Do you think I have enough seniority now to insist on better grub?'

'It's not seniority you need, Bill, it's a bloody gun.'

'This looks like Robbie Larch.' A Rover had just swept on to the pier.

Larch was about fifteen years older than Smellie, a square man gradually edging towards the spherical, red-faced and beady-eyed. He had a reputation for uninspired doggedness and a barely perceptible sense of humour. They had worked together briefly some years before and Smellie knew the other man's redeeming feature was his willingness to drive himself much harder than he drove his staff. One of his less endearing traits was his conviction that anyone born outwith a city boundary was a country bumpkin. He had been made Detective Superintendent just a year earlier. Smellie found it easy to tolerate him but difficult to like him.

They shook hands. 'Congratulations on your promotion, Bill. You're moving fast.' If there was any jealousy it was carefully hidden.

'Thanks, Robbie. The town's grown a lot over the past few years and we were seriously understaffed. I think that's why I was bumped up and the squad increased. This is Inspector Naismith. Jimmy, Mr Larch.'

'My inspector's following with one of the sergeants,' Larch said. 'Scene of Crime are on their way. What have you done so far?'

'Found and notified the dead woman's husband and arranged for formal identification once the body's been moved and made presentable. My squad are already started on tracking down her movements. Death is estimated at about eleven twenty last night, but we have to allow a generous window. And a pound coin dropped out of her mouth.'

'Knickers?'

'Not seen. But they may be in her shoulder bag.'

Larch shook his head, his face grim. 'They won't be. It's the same guy. God knows what he does with the knickers when he gets them home. Right, where is she?'

Behind him, another car arrived and more of Smellie's squad stepped out. 'I'll get them started on a house-to-house,' Smellie said. 'Jimmy will show you the body. And I've just spotted something.'

He pointed up at the wall of the main terminal building.

'CCTV!' Naismith said. 'We might get lucky.'

'I'll put someone on to that as well,' Smellie said.

Two white vans with flashing lights appeared at the entrance; Scene of Crime had arrived. Beyond them, on the far side of Shore Road, a crowd was collecting.

Smellie approached his squad and gave them a quick description of the situation without mentioning the missing panties or the pound coin.

'Anstruther, there are two CCTV cameras on the wall up there. Speak to the guy in that hut there, Walter Lapsley, and find out how we get to see the tapes. Cross and Langholm, you take the all-night café round the corner. Sandra Sim must have been well known in there, and she must have had friends she talked to. We need to know who they were and we need to know who she did business with last night and also on a regular basis. The rest of you spread out and speak to anyone who might have seen anything. Wherever there's a window overlooking this area, find whoever might have been behind that window between ten and one last night. Since the other murder was thirty miles away we have to assume there's a vehicle involved. I want to know every vehicle, from push bikes to artics, seen in this area last night. You know the drill, and you know my rules about keeping detailed notes.'

He paused.

'The indications are that we're dealing with a serial killer. If we miss something, other women may be murdered. No matter how wet and cold and miserable you get, bear that in mind at all times and stick with it. OK, let's get started.'

He watched them hurry away and looked up at the heavy grey clouds and the never-ending drizzle and felt a strange sense of dread.

2

The body was removed to the hospital a little before ten o'clock and the process of formal identification set in motion.

'Can we shift to the incident room now, Bill?' Larch said; he looked wet and cold. 'Scene of Crime can report to us there. I want to clue you in. Your inspector as well.'

As he drove the half-mile back along Shore Road with Larch and Naismith following in their own cars, Smellie smiled ruefully at the etiquette required of two officers of equal rank working on the same case in the bailiwick of the officer of fifteen years less seniority but fifteen years younger. It was a minefield. Larch clearly saw this as his case but he had to accept that Smellie's squad were doing most of the work. Professional courtesy required that anything he wanted done he had to ask for through Smellie. A direct order from Norman Fowler, that Larch was in charge, would have cleared the air.

The smaller conference room at the back of Divisional HQ had been converted to an incident room under the calm and efficient control of Inspector Sarah Noonan. Only Smellie knew that Sarah had recently been planniing to resign from the force when a miscarriage had changed everything. Her promotion had done a lot to remotivate her.

'We're still trying, Bill,' she had whispered when he offered his sympathy. 'You may not have me for long.'

'I don't want to lose you, Sarah, but I hope you succeed.' Jerry Noonan, the editor of the *Garrmouth Gazette* and Sarah's husband, had bought Smellie a celebratory whisky just a week previously. 'Tell Jerry I feel for him.'

'This is fine,' Larch said, looking round the room at the computers and rows of desks and tables, the blackboards and pegboards, the Ordnance Survey plans, the radios and mobiles on charge, the uniformed computer operators at their workstations, the air of organized bustle.

Smellie made the introductions. 'Inspector Noonan is our office manager, administration officer and action allocator. Whatever you need, she'll take care of it. And the coffee's good and the canteen's just along the corridor and we can send out.'

'Good.' Larch appeared barely interested in this trivia. He hung his sodden coat over a radiator. 'Let's talk. You too, Jimmy.'

They filled mugs with coffee and settled round one of the tables in the corner of the room. Larch produced a massive pipe and began stuffing tobacco into the bowl.

'You know about Karen Potter. Age nineteen, prostitute, a pretty girl, drank a bit but no habit. Lived with another girl in a tidy little flat. Strangled with a length of blue polypropylene rope at about ten forty-five on a Saturday night four weeks ago. The body was found lying among some bushes behind a row of lockup garages virtually within sight of Police HQ. No panties were found and there was a pound coin under her tongue. I've spent the past month hoping like hell it was a one-off, but all the time I knew it was too weird to be anything but one of a series.'

He snapped a cheap lighter and ignited the tobacco and tamped it down and fired it again. A cloud of blue smoke filled the air. Smellie sat back, seeking clean air. Naismith raised an eyebrow to Smellie and received a tiny nod and lit a cigarette.

'We kept the panties and the coin a secret,' Larch said. 'You know why. Prostitutes attract a lot of dafties who want the credit for killing one of them, or copycats who think someone just came up with a great idea. And there's always the problem of jokers and fake confessors. The senior investigating officer in each division was informed and instructed to sit on the information but keep an eye open. Now it's happened. Another murder, same MO, same details, thirty miles away from the first killing, and I am shit scared. I am haunted by the vision of Peter Sutcliffe.'

'What have you discovered so far?' Smellie asked.

Larch drank coffee noisily and pushed his pipe back into his mouth.

'We have interviewed four hundred and forty-five people, last I heard. We have viewed about sixty hours of CCTV again and again. We have knocked on every door of any relevance. We know every source of blue polypropylene rope in the town and neighbourhood and everyone who bought that kind of rope in the past five years, assuming they used a card or were recognized, and these people have been obliged to account for every last inch. Where a vehicle is traceable we have traced it. We have looked very closely at the dead girl's brother and father and two former boyfriends. We have looked very closely at every known sex offender of any kind still capable of breaking into a trot. We have tracked down twenty-one men who paid her for sex and we have leaned on them heavily. We have checked out her doctor and her landlord, and a guy who wanted to pimp for her, and the pubs where she drank, and the shops where she bought her clothes. We've gone back through the records looking for similar cases, or even cases only slightly similar, but found nothing. We've ruined the sex industry in the town. But we've no idea who killed her.'

'It may be easier now,' Naismith said. 'With a second murder.'

'God forgive me, Jimmy,' Larch said, 'but that's the way I'm thinking too. The more killings, the more information we get.'

'What was Karen Potter like as a person?' Smellie asked.

Larch sat back in his chair. 'We keep getting different pictures from different people. You know how it is. Her family and the girl she shared a flat with are eager to find excuses for her; other people are less sympathetic; both her ex-boyfriends are pretty bitter. The descriptions range from gutsy through misused to spiteful. Everyone had a different point of view.'

'What do you think?'

'I think she was a pretty kid without much between the ears who wanted money and used her charms to earn it,' Larch said. 'She wasn't planning to make a career out of it. Her flatmate told me they had this dream of earning enough money to open a shop. A florist's shop or a dress shop or a video shop. Seems the dream changed from day to day.'

Naismith stubbed out his cigarette. 'Was her friend a working girl?'

'No. She works behind the ticket counter at the railway station. But she doesn't like her job.'

Smellie sat back even further, trying to escape the blue smoke. 'Have Forensic come up with anything?'

Larch nodded but showed no enthusiasm. 'Stuff which may help us prove something once we catch the bastard, but nothing to help us do that. The rope was cut with a sharp blade, probably a Stanley knife. The bit we found two weeks ago is exactly like the bit we found today – about three feet long, with two half-hitches at each end to stop fraying and provide a grip. Polypropylene is a good choice, incidentally – it's very strong and it doesn't shed fibres like some ropes. And it's very common; there must be miles of the bloody stuff in the county. What was found on it were traces of soil and dried vegetation, root material mainly. That's been gone into in great detail, but the traces are very common in these parts. Just about any bit of rope that's been lying on the ground will carry similar traces. All Forensic will say is that if we find another bit of rope with the same combination it will probably be from the same source. We took plaster casts of no less than seven different footprints in the immediate area, and we've managed to eliminate four of these, which leaves us with three unknowns, all of them too indistinct to be any use in court. We have failed completely to come up with a witness. An appeal for information in the papers and on television produced a very small response, none of it useful.'

'Anything else? Anything on the body?'

Larch shook his head. 'The indications are there was no sex act. The view is there was an attempt, a bit of groping and so on, clothing loosened, but no actual act. So no traces. Karen Potter was found lying face down, skirt up round her waist, no panties, like Sandra Sim. And, just like Sandra Sim, her stockings were disturbed, probably by the killer pulling off her panties.'

'So maybe he tried but couldn't get it up and got angry,' Naismith said.

'That's one assessment, Jimmy,' Larch said. 'I'm not convinced.'

'He'd bought the rope and cut it and knotted it,' Smellie said. 'In other words, he went out intending to kill someone. I think we need a psychological profile.'

'Agreed,' Larch said. 'I'll arrange that. Can we link your computers to ours at HQ so you can read what we've logged so far?'

'Sarah will do that, Robbie; all she needs is your authority and someone to speak to at HQ.'

'I'll see to that. Bill, I want to bring my squad in. I want to saturate the town.'

'Let's do that, Robbie,' Smellie said. 'And let's start looking for a pattern. Both murders happened on a Saturday night, within half an hour or so of each other, but thirty miles and four weeks apart. Why was the killer in these two separate places at the same time on the same night four weeks apart, doing the same thing to similar women? Was it just to commit murder, or was there an incidental reason?'

Larch's beady eyes narrowed to slits. 'How do you mean?'

'I mean,' Smellie said, 'was our man maybe also a football supporter following his team, or a rugby supporter? Maybe a player. What events were common to both towns on the relevant dates? Pub quizzes, line dancing, golf matches, art exhibitions: there are lots of possibilities.'

'Yes. Good, Bill,' Larch's attitude changed perceptibly, as if he had suddenly realized that Smellie's promotion had been earned. 'By the way, something I should have said, but I'd forgotten – there's a noticeable physical similarity between the two women. They're years apart in age, but they were both tall-ish and slim and had a lot of black hair and were attractive. And they were both wearing black stockings. Maybe our man's got a fixation about women like that. Maybe a woman like that had a bad effect on him once. Maybe it's some kind of revenge thing.'

Smellie nodded. 'We definitely need a psychological profile.'

He glanced round and saw various members of his staff obviously waiting to speak to him. 'Let's hear what's been discovered so far.' He pointed to DC Anstruther and beckoned him over. The constable approached, bringing with him a tall man with brown hair fringing a shiny scalp.

'You asked me to check out the CCTV, sir. This is Mr Beale, the ferry terminal manager. Mr Beale, Detective Superintendent Smellie.'

Smellie rose and shook hands. 'Thank you for coming along,

Mr Beale. Sit down, please. You too, Anstruther. What do you have for us?'

Beale reached into the game pockets of his dripping Barbour jacket and produced four video tapes and placed them on the table.

'To explain, ah, Detective Super—'

'Mister works fine, sir. Saves time.'

'To explain, Mr Smellie: we have four cameras covering the ferry terminal, one at each corner of the main building. They're in place in the hope of reducing pilfering and vandalism and, I must say, since we installed them, there has been a marked drop in the amount of goods going missing. It was quite expensive to set them up. . . .'

'Do they run all the time?' Larch demanded.

'Oh, yes,' Beale said. 'They move back and forward, you see, and everyone knows they're there, and they have an effect. . . .'

'Let's view them,' Smellie said.

They congregated round a set in a corner.

'The constable said the one showing the gate and the south pier is what you really want to see,' Beale said. 'It covers the twenty-four hours from noon on Saturday to noon today except, of course, I've interrupted the usual sequence. . . .'

'Thank you, sir,' Anstruther said, taking a firm grip on the tape and removing it from Beale's grasp; he loaded it and set it to play. The screen showed snow then settled down to a poor quality black and white picture of the pier and one of the ferries.

'The camera doesn't run continuously,' Beale said. 'It's set to take a shot every two seconds, so everything's a bit jerky.'

They watched figures and vehicles move up and down the quay in sudden jumps. The camera panned right until it covered Shore Road and the roofs of the wooden huts then began to reverse its travel. The time and date in the corner of the screen indicated noon on the Saturday.

'Fast forward it, Anstruther,' Smellie said, then turned to the ferry terminal manager.

'Thank you, Mr Beale. We're hoping this may help us with our enquiries.'

'What exactly has happened, Mr Smellie? All I got from Walter Lapsley was that a woman had been found dead behind one of our huts.'

'You have the whole story, sir.'

'Are we definitely talking murder?'

'Yes, sir. Were you aware that at least one of the local prostitutes used your huts as a convenient place to take her clients?'

Beale hesitated. Under the Barbour jacket he seemed to be very properly dressed in white shirt and tie and pressed trousers.

'This is rather embarrassing. Various members of the staff had mentioned it and, of course, the evidence is there on the tapes. But it hardly seemed something I need get involved in. Really, the prostitutes working around the docks are a police problem, not mine. I have enough to do without all that.'

'Very true, sir. How long do you keep your tapes?'

'We have two sets,' Beale said. 'We take one set out and replace them with the other set and hold the first set for twenty-four hours. If there's no problem, the tapes are switched at the end of the next twenty-four hours and taped over. We have a spare set we've never used yet, so you can hold on to these ones for the time being.'

'Thank you for your assistance, sir.'

Beale realized he was being dismissed and left. Anstruther hit a button.

'Got it, sir. I've stopped it at eleven o'clock last night.'

'Run it.'

In the darkness, the picture quality was very poor. The quay was inadequately lit and it was only when the camera swung round to show Shore Road that they could see anything at all clearly. Vehicles jerked past, headlights blurring the image; dark figures made their way at intervals in and out of the street lights and the glow from various windows. Two women appeared at the entrance to the ferry terminal then vanished as the camera panned back down the pier.

'Was that Sandra Sim?' Smellie said. 'The one on the right. Anstruther, take a note of what's happening and the times off the screen.'

'Come on,' Larch muttered impatiently as the camera reached the end of its travel and began its intermittent journey back up the wet cobbles to Shore Road. When it reached its limit there was no one in sight at the corner. The next time it showed Shore Road there were the same two women silhouetted at the corner, one of them leaning against the wall.

The group watched the sequence of pictures in silence. According to the numbers flickering past in the bottom corner of the screen it took the camera one and a half minutes to complete a full traverse from any given point to the same point.

'In my experience,' Larch muttered, 'there is nothing so ball-aching as watching CCTV.'

'There!' Anstruther exclaimed, pointing.

They watched what was probably Sandra Sim and a man crossing the cobbles towards the wooden buildings and vanish. They returned twelve minutes later. The man disappeared round the corner at the café and Sandra Sim stopped and there was a momentary flash of light as she lit a cigarette.

'Eleven twenty-six,' Naismith said.

'That Land Rover is still parked at the other side of Shore Road,' Smellie said. 'It arrived about ten minutes ago.'

The camera made its slow traverse and returned. There was no sign of Sandra Sim. It made another four traverses before they saw her again.

'Yes!' Naismith burst out.

Two figures, Sandra Sim and a man, were frozen three times as they crossed the gap between the corner at the café and the wooden huts. The squat figure of the other woman showed in the first shot then vanished.

'Eleven thirty-two,' Naismith said.

They waited tensely. Starting at 11.41 they saw three indistinct images of the man walking back from the wooden huts to the corner then the camera swung away. When it had repeated its traverse the Land Rover at the far side of Shore Road was no longer there.

'We have to talk to that guy,' Larch muttered.

They watched the tape intently for a long time.

'Twelve forty,' Smellie said, 'and we haven't seen Sandra Sim for about an hour. I think Henry Jenning's estimate was accurate. And I think we may have seen our man and probably his vehicle. Anstruther, find out if we can have these images enhanced. Jimmy, someone should view the other tapes as well, just in case we can get another look at that Land Rover. Arrange that, then get people on to identifying that other woman, the one who was talking to Sandra Sim. Put Cross and Langholm in charge of that: they've done the groundwork at the all-night café and she's very likely another prostitute.'

He paused for a moment. 'I know the police don't run CCTV in Garrmouth but maybe someone else in the town does.'

'Tesco and Asda both do, sir,' Anstruther said. 'Asda had theirs installed a couple of months back. I just happened to notice. There may be other cameras I don't know about.'

'Well done, lad,' Smellie said. 'I want to know about all the cameras in the town and what they show for last night. If you need more help, just ask.'

Sarah Noonan approached the table and caught Smellie's attention.

'Newbold called in, sir. He's been approached by a Miss Willingshaw. She was with Sandra Sim just before she vanished. He's bringing her in.'

'Belay that last order, Jimmy,' Smellie said. 'We just got lucky.'

3

Smellie looked at Larch. 'Robbie, does anything you've seen today give you any new ideas?'

'Not a bloody thing, Bill.'

'But you're convinced both murders were carried out by the same man?'

'Definitely.'

'Not a woman?'

Larch stared at him, the red face frozen. 'No. I don't see it as a woman.'

'We'll see what the squad have dug up.'

The results so far were not encouraging. DC Marianne Cross and DC Langholm had made a nuisance of themselves at the all-night café but it had been difficult.

'It's run by Theo and Thelma Leaver,' Langholm said. 'A hard working couple, you could say, if not exactly hygienic, but their regulars are working women and truckers, men off the ferries, drunks and pimps and druggies and they make a point of not seeing anything. They sell tea and coffee and vile food and keep their eyes and ears shut.'

'But you persisted,' Smellie said. 'I've taught you how to persist.'

'Yes, sir,' Marianne Cross said. 'I got Thelma on her own and applied a bit of pressure and a bit of sympathy and she eventually opened up. She knew Sandra Sim, of course. The lady's territory was the few yards from the café door to the entrance to the ferry terminal and her hours were about eight o'clock to one or two o'clock in the morning, depending on the day of the week and the way the ferries were operating. She'd do the business in the cab of a truck, or the back of a car, or somewhere in the ferry complex. I presume that means where her body was found. Mrs Leaver didn't have the details.'

'Good, well done,' Smellie said. 'What about regulars?'

'We have just three names,' Langholm said. 'A guy off one of the ferries, a truck driver and the manager of the Harbour Bar. First name only on the driver.'

'What about vehicles?'

'They say they can't see much from inside the café, especially at night, and we think that's true, sir. The front window is small and dirty and most of the time it's running with condensation.'

'Did they see Sandra Sim last night?'

'Several times,' Langholm said, checking his notebook. 'She went in for a cup of tea at about ten, got talking to a man and they went out together. She came back about half an hour later with another prostitute, first name Avril, for more tea, then went out again, then back some time towards eleven for more tea, then out again. Alone. We worked hard on that part, sir, with the Leaver couple, since that was the last sighting of the dead woman, but that's it. Last seen some time after eleven, leaving the Harbour Café, alone.'

'The people there at this time of the day are not the ones who are there late on a Saturday night, sir,' Cross said. 'We have some names or nicknames, no firm addresses, but there were people the Leavers didn't recognize. They get a lot of drunks when the pubs shut, plus truckers and weirdoes. The both displayed a complete lack of curiosity about their customers. Self-defence, probably.'

'Speak to Inspector Noonan,' Smellie said. 'Tell her I want all these people tracked down and questioned. Tell her Mr Larch's squad are on their way so we'll have the manpower.'

DC Newbold had entered the incident room with a short but seriously plump young woman in a patterned headsquare and yellow anorak.

'That could be the woman off the video,' Larch whispered. 'The one at the corner with Sandra Sim.'

Smellie rose as they approached.

'Avril Willingshaw, sir,' Newbold said. 'She approached me in Shore Street; she says she may be able to help.'

'Hello, Miss Willingshaw. Sit down, please. Have you given this officer your full name and address?'

'Yes, sir.' Avril Willingshaw perched on the chair, her toes barely touching the floor, skirt stretched tight over hefty thighs. She seemed to be in her early twenties but looked younger. The baby face and untidy curls gave her a certain charm, but it was spoiled when she opened her mouth to reveal teeth badly in need of attention.

'You were a friend of Sandra Sim?'

'Yes, sir. We both hung around the caff, like.'

'Sandra Sim was a prostitute. Are you? I'm not interested in what you do, but I need to know.'

'Yes, sir.'

'Good. And you know what has happened to her?'

Avril Willingshaw nodded and her eyes filled with tears. 'She's been murdered. That's what I heard. Round the huts.'

'That's correct. And we're trying to find who killed her and that's why I need you to tell me everything that happened last night, everyone you saw, in as much detail as possible. You'll be giving a statement, which will be recorded so we don't forget anything. We'll go through to the interview room, where it's quieter. Before we go through, I want you to look at a video.'

Avril Willingshaw confirmed that she was the woman seen in the video with Sandra Sim and that she had not seen Sandra Sim after about 11.30. Anstruther had already noted precise times from the video and gave Smellie a photocopy. Smellie and Naismith took her through to one of the interview rooms, leaving Larch to detail his own squad. Naismith switched on the recorder and explained Avril Willingshaw's rights to her.

'Right, Miss Willingshaw,' Smellie said. 'We're specially interested in the period around eleven o'clock, but we'd better take it from when you arrived for work on Saturday night. When was that?'

'About eight o'clock, sir.'

Half an hour later Smellie was wishing he had told her to start from ten o'clock. Avril Willingshaw had a fine memory for trivia but no instinct for relevance. He let her ramble on in the hope that something important might appear.

'Then there wasn't much happening for a while around eleven o'clock but we was just waiting for the pubs to shut but it was peeing down which is never good for trade. Me and Sandra was chatting at the corner when this van stops across the road and we think, here we go, but nothing happens. Then this other bloke comes up and she takes him round the huts, so I goes across to the van but he wasn't interested.'

Smellie stared at her. This incident must have happened while the camera had panned away from Shore Road. 'You spoke to him?'

'Yeah. The usual, and he said no thanks.'

'Tell me everything you can about him, please.'

Avril Willingshaw put her hands to her mouth. She had fat little fingers with grubby nails.

'Was it him?'

'Could be. What did he look like?'

Her round eyes stared at Smellie. 'I don't know. He was just a shape and it was dark inside the van. He had his collar up and a hat on.'

The last man seen with Sandra Sim in the video had been wearing some kind of short coat or an anorak and what looked like a soft hat with the brim turned down.

'Did you notice anything else? His accent, for instance?'

'All he said was, "No, thanks". I didn't notice nothing odd about the way he said it. Except, he didn't sound common, like.'

'Local or a visitor?'

'I'd say local.'

'White or coloured?'

'I don't know. Yes, I do. I saw his hand. White.'

'Was there anyone else in the van?'

'No. Unless there was someone hiding in back.'

'Did you smell anything? Tobacco, aftershave, anything at all?'

Thinking was a slow process for Avril Willingshaw, requiring heavy breathing and a furrowed brow.

'Smoke, yeah. Cigarette smoke.'

'Any name on the side of the van?'

'No. I'd have noticed that.'

'What make of van was it?'

'A Land Rover. And I didn't memorize the number, if you're going to ask.'

'Go on, please.'

'Well, that's it. My feet were wet and I was cold so I went in for a cuppa, then my friend from the Harbour Bar come over and me and him went back to his place for the night. Then I come out this morning and everybody's talking and I hear what's happened to Sandra and I went to one of the policemen and said maybe I can help.'

'You have helped, Miss Willingshaw,' Smellie said. 'Thank you.'

*

He gave Larch an abbreviated account of Avril Willingshaw's story.

'It tallies with what we saw on the video, with the extra bit we didn't see. Naismith's arranging a search of the road where the Land Rover was parked in case there's a cigarette end, a packet, anything at all. And we'll be asking everyone in the area if they saw the vehicle.'

'It's our best lead, Bill. Your man Anstruther has gone off to HQ to get the tape copied then the original will go to London for enhancement. If we can type the vehicle and get the number we'll be well ahead.'

Smellie frowned. 'I'm visualizing the video. The vehicle was parked right under a street light, which left the interior in darkness and the number plates in shadow. That may have been deliberate. And when he switched on the headlights and drove away, the glare would mask the plates.'

'Leave me a little hope to work on, Bill. I'm depressed enough as it is.'

'Sorry, Robbie.'

Sarah Noonan caught Smellie's eye. 'The Press are arriving. Can you speak to them? They're already talking serial killer.'

'Half an hour, in the front hall.'

Scene of Crime arrived fifteen minutes later. Sergeant Mary Goodison, Smellie and Larch met round the table with more coffee.

'Desperately little to tell you, sir,' Goodison said, talking to Smellie as senior investigating officer for the division, but clearly aware that Larch was involved through the previous murder. 'I did the Karen Potter job as well. Same type of rope, same length to within a few millimetres, same knots. The lab will decide if the same knife was used to cut the rope. Strangulation appears to have been the only assault, but there are a couple of marks on her legs where she probably kicked herself while she was struggling. The rope was passed round her neck from behind and drawn tight. There was no knot in the rope apart from the half-hitches at the ends. She made a serious attempt at getting her fingers under the rope to relieve the pressure, but failed. The result is seven scratches on the front of her throat above the ligature. I expect the lab will find traces of her own skin under her nails. The mark of the ligature is clearly visible, and there's only one mark, which usually indicates a competent strangler and a reasonably quick death. You'll get the details on that after the post-mortem.'

'Was there sex immediately before the murder?' Larch asked.

'That will be a hard one to answer, sir, with her being a prostitute. If she'd had a customer earlier in the evening. . . .' Mary Goodison shrugged.

'What about her clothes?' Smellie asked.

'Her blouse was open as far as the navel, sir, and her bra had been pulled up to reveal her breasts. No panties, as you saw. I got the feeling the man may have asked her to turn round, maybe pretending he liked it that way, so he could get the rope round her neck without her being able to get at him with her hands.'

'Any evidence that she was actually wearing panties? They don't always.'

'There's a mark on her right hip, sir, a sort of scrape, which makes me think her panties were pulled off her after she was killed. The way her stockings were disarranged confirms that possibility. As if they'd been disturbed when he pulled down her panties.'

Robbie Larch was writing busily in his notebook. 'Same as last time.'

'Yes, sir.'

'Go on.'

'There's not much else, sir. The pound coin will go to the lab, in the hope that there may be a print. The only surfaces at the locus that would take a print are the various windows, so we dusted them. We searched the ground, of course, but from what I hear she'd been taking men round there for a long time so what we found won't be specific. No clear footprints, because the ground is cobbled, same as the rest of the pier. A few cigarette packets and condom packets and cigarette ends. A lot of used condoms under the huts and down a drain. We took plenty of traces of fibres off the wooden walls, and the lab will report on these, but I suspect they'll just give you a lot of work to do and nothing to show for it, unless you find someone and get a match. Everything relevant is already on its way to the lab.'

'Thanks, Sergeant,' Larch said. He was clearly disappointed. 'What now?'

Smellie held up a note passed to him by one of the uniformed computer operators.

'The post-mortem started a few minutes ago.'

'What about the Press?'

'They'll have to wait.'

Smellie and Larch entered the pathology room wearing the green plastic aprons and surgical gloves and found Henry Jennings and a woman already at work on the naked body lying on the stainless steel table. Two technicians from Forensic were packing the dead woman's clothing into evidence bags.

Larch pointed to the tall woman with the untidy greying hair. 'Bill, do you know Professor Shane?'

'No, although I've heard the name.'

'She's the best,' Jennings said. 'She's streets ahead of me.'

The grey hair is misleading, Smellie thought; she can't be

more than forty. She was a lean and attractive woman with lively grey eyes.

'So you're the coming man in Garrmouth Division, Detective Superintendent Smellie. What do I call you?'

'Bill will do nicely.'

'Never think of changing your name? Smellie must be a bit of a drawback.'

'It's my dad's name.'

'But what do women say?'

'They say, I'll live with you but I don't want to be Mrs Smellie. And I never even got that far with a girl called Ellie. What do I call you?'

'Leonora. Really. So now you can get your own back. Henry likes you, which is good enough for me. Any suspects?'

'None so far,' Smellie said. 'We're waiting for your report, hoping you'll give us something definite to work on.'

'Don't think so, dear. Everything points to a swift and efficient strangulation by ligature. The windpipe is occluded and there's clear evidence of petechial haemorrhaging. I'd say the strangler was strong, with a strong grip: he was able to create sufficient pressure to cause the collapse of the windpipe and also the constriction of the large blood vessels without having to go for a second attempt. The single line of bruising indicates that. That led to unconsciousness due to cerebral hypoxia, followed by death due to asphyxia. It's more complicated than that, but I've learned to simplify things for policemen. The victim had drunk alcohol during the hour before death. I can smell bitter lemon, so it was probably vodka. And quite a lot of tea. It'll all be in my report.'

'How long would it take?' Smellie asked. 'For Sandra Sim to die?'

'Maybe a bit more than two minutes. If you'd managed to grab your man within half an hour of the murder you'd have found the marks of the rope on his hands. It took a lot of effort.'

Smellie looked at Larch, but the older man appeared to have nothing to say.

'Any sign of semen or anal penetration?'

'No.'

'Any other injuries? Any indication of assault?'

'No. A couple of marks on her legs, almost certainly the result of her kicking herself while she was struggling.'

'Was she a user?'

'Not by injection. Tell you later if she sniffed or smoked.'

Smellie studied the dead face for the first time. Sandra Sim had died at the age of thirty-five. Clear complexion, regular features, straight nose, a mouth which must have been quite shapely and inviting in life. It was impossible to discern anything from the closed eyes, but she must have been an attractive woman. The breasts were not large but they were well shaped and firm. The black hair would have hung down below her shoulders, probably naturally straight but artificially waved.

Smellie bent to look at the seven distinct scratches on the neck above the clear mark of the ligature.

'You've checked the fingernails for residue, of course.'

'They've been scraped, Bill.'

He nodded. 'We'll have to go. If you want, when you're finished, come along to the incident room at Divisional HQ. We have good coffee.'

'I'm hungry.'

'If I'm there I'll buy you lunch.'

'A gentleman. I've found a gentleman. Life takes on a new meaning.'

'And you can let me know everything you've learned.'

'Maybe not all that much of a gentleman.'

'She a lively sort,' Smellie said as he and Larch went back up the stairs.

'What you see is what you get,' Larch said. 'And I reckon you could have her if you wanted. She has a bit of a reputation. I think I should talk to the Press, if you don't mind, Bill. I already spoke to them about the first murder. Several times.'

'You're welcome to that job. They love a serial killer: they're going to be at us like flies round a corpse. Is that an unfortunate simile?'

'It's accurate,' Larch said.

4

Robbie Larch had struggled into his damp raincoat and gone back out to see what was happening on site. Smellie followed DS Grossmith along the corridor to one of the interview rooms.

'He broke down when he had to identify his wife, sir, but he's all right now, pretty well.'

'Did he have anything relevant to offer?'

'No, sir. His wife left home at about eight o'clock last night, as usual, and the next time he saw her was on the slab. We have his statement.'

'Let's not crowd him. I'll talk to him alone.'

Arnold Sim sat hunched on the hard chair, arms spread before him on the table, a cigarette smouldering between stained fingers. He did not look up when Smellie entered and sat down.

'Mr Sim, I'm Detective Superintendent Smellie of Garrmouth Division. First of all, may I offer my sincere condolences.'

Arnold Sim nodded but did not look up. He had the air of a man drained of the life force. The thinning dark hair was neatly parted, the narrow face grey and hollow; his shirt was clean, his tie neatly knotted, the dark suit in good condition, but he still managed to project a sense of being vaguely unsavoury.

'Thanks. You lot didn't do much of a job of protecting her.'

There was an unpleasant whine in his voice; Smellie remembered Naismith's description of this man as 'a sleazy little toerag'.

'Tell me about your wife, Mr Sim. I know you've made a statement, but it would help me if you could fill in some background information.'

Sim dropped his cigarette end into an empty mug. 'What do you want to know?'

'Tell me what she was like as a person. When did you meet her?'

Sim sniffed wetly. 'I had this business going years ago, selling stuff round the open-air markets. Sandra and her dad had a stall, selling jeans and sweatshirts and like that. We started seeing each other, then she got pregnant and we got married and the wee boy was born. He's twelve now. Then I got sick with this kidney trouble. We tried to carry on, but I was no bloody use and we got into debt all over the place and couldn't pay the rent. Then all the debts got cleared and I discovered Sandra'd been working down the docks. On the game. Discovering your wife's had to go on the game because you're a useless article doesn't do much for your self-respect, but secretly you're glad of the money and after a while you get used to idea. God knows how we'll manage now.'

'She stayed with you,' Smellie said, prompting him.

Sim nodded and lit another cigarette. 'She was a good wife and mother and kept the house neat and clean and never once said nothing to blame me for her having to sell herself on the street. And the lad goes to school every day in a clean shirt and a blazer and he's learning French and mathematics and computers and his teachers say he's very bright.'

He suddenly looked Smellie straight in the eye for the first time.

'You found a dead prostitute and what did you think?'

Smellie nodded. 'I certainly didn't think a tidy house and a boy in a clean shirt and a blazer, learning French. I know better now.'

'Catch the bastard, mister. Lock him up.'

'Help me. Did your wife say anything about any kind of trouble recently? Some screwball, some guy she thought might be dangerous?'

'A lot of them scared her. Drunks and druggies and weirdos. But she didn't mention anyone special recently. We never talked much about it. Maybe one of the other girls might know something.'

'We're working on that. When you gave your statement, did you mention any friends she had who might know something?'

Sim nodded. 'Three or four.'

'Good. We'll talk to them. Did she use drugs at all? Could there have been a problem with someone selling drugs?'

'No. She wasn't into that stuff. She took a drink, but not drugs.'

'One last thing. She'd had a drink during the evening. Can you make a guess at where she would have gone to get it?'

'The Harbour Bar.'

'Right.' Smellie rose. 'I'll arrange a lift home for you. We'll get this guy, Mr Sim. We'll put him away for life.'

'You do that. You owe Sandra that. She was a good woman.'

Smellie returned to the incident room and beckoned to DC Newbold.

'See what you can find out about the dead woman's husband, Arnold Sim. On the quiet. How things were between him and his wife, where he drinks, where he was last night, what the word is in the neighbourhood.'

Smellie and Naismith stood at the ferry entrance in the drizzle. Naismith's corduroy cap was saturated but his anorak seemed to be keeping him dry. The knees of his trousers were wet but his large brown shoes were equal to the struggle.

'I hadn't realized there were so many people living up there,' Naismith said, nodding towards the peeling stone buildings on the far side of Shore Road. 'I should have, I suppose, but somehow you never raise your eyes above street level.'

'It's news to me too, Jimmy,' Smellie said, surveying the rows of windows above the shops and small businesses at street level. Most of the buildings were four storeys high. 'Have we learned anything?'

'I've lost track,' Naismith said. 'I'm beginning to understand why you spend so much time reading the reports on the computer into the small hours. It's the only way to sort things out. But I've told everyone to come back to me if they learn anything interesting, and the only response I've had so far is from Sly. He talked to an old guy on the third floor at the corner of Shore Road and Ferry Road, up there. He recognized Sandra Sim from the photo. He'd seen her often enough. I think he spends his time spying on what's happening down here.'

'What did he say?'

'He saw her go round the huts three times during the evening, but he went to bed about half past eleven and he's vague about the time. He may have seen Sandra Sim with the murderer, but it may have been the customer before that and his descriptions are useless. He's in his eighties and would not make a good witness. He didn't tell us anything we didn't already know.'

'Talk to him yourself, Jimmy; get what you can. And get someone to check at the Harbour Bar: Sandra Sim probably had a drink there during the evening. Anything from the search where the van was parked?'

'A pile of fag ends, all wet and soggy. Two fag packets, also wet and soggy and run over by vehicles. An empty coke can. The remains of a fish supper. A pool of vomit. Everything's gone to the lab. I'm not optimistic: there's a helluva lot of litter in this street.'

'What about people who might have seen the van?'

'It's the usual problem: most of the people here now are not the people who were here late on Saturday night. Anyway, no one we've found yet. No one in the neighbourhood owns or drives a Land Rover van. We're still working on it.'

Smellie's mobile sounded.

'DC Cooper, sir. I've been viewing these videos, the three which don't show the site of the murder, and I think I may have found something, although it's hard to make out.'

'Tell me what you've seen.'

'I concentrated on the possible time of the murder, sir, and there's a long wheelbase Land Rover turning off Shore Road into Palmerston Place at the Marine Hotel at about the right time.'

'Well done. Can you identify the registration number?'

'No, sir. Lousy picture and too much glare from the lights.'

'Arrange to have that video copied at HQ then sent to London for enhancement. Anstruther will tell you how.'

'He's with me now, sir. He wants to talk to you.'

'Put him on.'

'Lavery and I have been looking at the Tesco and Asda videos, sir,' Anstruther said. 'The Tesco one's useless: all it shows is the car-park and the back of the store, and of course it's at the wrong end of the town. The Asda one also shows the junction of the High Street and Ferry Road, but the only Land Rover seen anywhere near the relevant time is a short wheelbase estate. And that was more than an hour before the murder.'

'OK. Any more cameras in the town?'

'There are two covering the out-of-town shopping area at the north end, sir. Front and back of the DIY superstore and Halfords and Comet and so on. Do you want me to follow that up?'

'Not relevant. Any others?'

'No, sir.'

'Right. Well done, Anstruther. Thank you.'

Robbie Larch approached, his sparse hair plastered to his head by the rain. He looked thoroughly depressed.

'Anything?'

Smellie brought him up to date. 'I think the best bet is the videos.' He pointed along Shore Road. 'That's the corner with Palmerston Place at the Marine Hotel. The camera's on the far corner of the terminal building here. There's just a chance that when the Land Rover turned the corner the camera may have picked up the registration number, even if Cooper can't identify it for the moment. It'll be enhanced.'

Larch sneezed explosively. 'You keep rotten bloody weather in this town, Bill.'

'It's very pleasant in the summer.'

'I'll come back then, with my bucket and spade.'

He wandered off and Smellie looked round at the ferry complex.

'Has someone spoken to this Walter Lapsley, the guy who found the body?'

Naismith nodded. 'We got his statement. He'd gone home. He's pretty badly shocked.'

'Anything suspicious?'

'He seems kosher. He's in his early sixties, a dried-up little runt, active in his parish church, married with two grown-up children. One of his daughters was visiting yesterday evening, with her husband and the grandchild.'

'Did they stay overnight?'

'Yes. They'd come down from Durham. They had a fancy meal at home and watched videos of the baby. And he drives a Micra. I don't see him as a suspect.'

'Good. Let's walk. There's a ferry due in later today, isn't there?'

'Three o'clock.'

They found George Beale in a dark-brown, first-floor office with a long window looking out to sea.

'Come in, Mr Smellie. I'm not usually here on a Sunday, but I thought it would be better if I were available, under the circumstances.' On his own territory he seemed much more self-confident.

'This is Inspector Naismith,' Smellie said. 'I don't think you were introduced earlier. We're familiarizing ourselves with the scene of the crime. Were any of your people at work here last night?'

Beale waved them to chairs at a heavy wooden table and sat down.

'There's no one here overnight. Hence the cameras. We used to have a night watchman but he drank a bit and was no use at all.'

'And there are no windows overlooking the wooden huts and the entrance?'

'No. Everything points out to sea.'

Smellie nodded. The office was very quiet, everything in it neat and orderly. 'How long have you worked here?'

'All my life.' Beale smiled fondly. 'Started as the most junior assistant in the payroll section and worked my way up. Passed my exams, kept my nose clean, outlasted the rest of the staff and eventually became manager.'

Smellie responded with a smile of his own. 'It seems at least some of your seagoing employees are familiar with the ladies who work along Shore Road. Do you know anything about that?'

Beale nodded. 'I've been told it happens. None of my business, of course, and I couldn't name anyone. If it's of any help to you, both ships were at sea last night. Which raises a matter I was going to phone you about – we have a ferry due in at three o'clock. Will your cars and the black and yellow tape and all these policemen still be here at that time? I mean, I have to give some thought to the company's image and so on. . . .'

'They'll be gone by that time,' Smellie said. He indicated the computer on Beale's desk. 'Can you provide a printout showing the names and addresses of all your employees?'

'Of course. I can give you a complete alphabetical list, or I can break it down into seagoing and shore, which might be more useful to you.'

'That's great, Mr Beale,' Smellie said. 'And any information you have about people on leave, or sick, or otherwise not in their usual locations would be helpful. We'll need that for last night and also for the Saturday evening four weeks ago.'

The extra bodies from HQ had occupied the big tables in the incident room; extra computers had been brought in from somewhere and were networked to Police HQ in Brickhill. Smellie, Naismith, Larch and his detective inspector, Stewart Pearce, met round the desk in Smellie's office. It was now almost seven o'clock in the evening, dark outside, and they were all tired and wet, their faces marked by the wind and the rain. Smellie had suggested a meal but Larch had wanted a conference first.

Smellie used the phone. 'Sarah, who's co-ordinating the vehicle sightings?'

'Barry, sir.'

'Tell him to come in with whatever he's got, and ask him to bring four coffees as well. Who's working on the list of local events?'

'Anstruther, sir.'

'I'll want him in when I'm finished with Barry.'

Larch's face was going scarlet as the heat of the office brought the blood back to his skin. Smellie could feel his own ears tingling. They sat in tired silence, Larch loading his pipe, until the door opened and DS Barry entered with a tray and a pile of computer printout paper.

'Join us, Barry,' Smellie said, and made the introductions. Promoting Barry to detective sergeant had been forced on him; Winston would have been his personal choice. Anstruther had the intelligence but not the experience.

Larch fired his pipe. Naismith looked at Smellie, received a fatalistic nod and lit a cigarette.

'Have we identified the Land Rover yet, Barry?' Smellie asked.

'Not definitely, sir. We found seven people who remember it but only vaguely, and another two who actually had their eyes open. One said it was a van, the other said it was an estate. Neither could say if it was long or short wheelbase. Neither bothered to look at the registration number, not even the year letter. They both thought it was green.'

'We know it's a van from the videos,' Larch said. 'There can't be all that many Land Rover vans.'

Barry indicated the sheets of printout paper. 'I have a list of all the properly registered Land Rover vans in the county. There are six hundred and seventy-five of them. And the one we're looking for may be from outwith the county.'

They all went silent. 'Shit!' Larch muttered.

'It gives us something to work on,' Pearce said. He was a thin man of about forty, fair-haired and handsome, very smartly dressed. He looked a question at Larch and received a nod.

'The vehicle's your job, Stewart. Find out first if the lab has managed to enhance the videos, then get someone to go back through the videos from the first murder. We weren't looking specifically for Land Rovers. Maybe something will show. This is our only lead, so take all the bodies you can get hold of.'

'Thanks, Barry,' Smellie said. 'Send Anstruther in, please.'

Someone's stomach rumbled. 'Sorry,' Naismith said insincerely.

'I'm hungry too,' Smellie said, hoping Larch would rise to the bait. 'We'll get a bite when we're finished here.'

Anstruther came in. His spots were clearing up and he still seemed to vibrate with energy and eagerness.

'Sit down, Anstruther,' Smellie said. 'You were looking for a pattern, some reason for our murderer being in two places thirty miles apart on Saturday nights four weeks apart at about the same time.'

'Yes, sir.' Anstruther looked round the intent faces of his superiors and blushed nervously. 'I haven't finished yet, sir. I keep finding new possibilities. With both murders being on a Saturday, there are an astonishing number of leisure events taking place. But Garrmouth United were playing at home the first Saturday and in London yesterday, so that appears to be irrelevant. Both the first and second rugby teams were at home both Saturdays, which doesn't make sense of a murder thirty miles away. There was motor cycle scrambling at Chapel Edge both Saturdays, and that's roughly equidistant between the two towns. However, there's been scrambling there every weekend since September.' He sighed. 'I've looked at field archery, shooting, rambling, cinemas, theatres, art exhibitions, museums, car auctions, folk concerts, a whole load of stuff. If our man is looking for a second-hand car or likes museums or art exhibitions he could have been in both towns on the appropriate date. If he just wanted to see the latest films he needn't have left the county town, unless, of course, he wanted to see two of the new movies and missed one because he only has Saturday nights free and had to come here to see it. The time of the murders would tie in with him getting out of a cinema. I'm sorry, sir, I know that's a bit vague, but it's very difficult to be specific. I'd like more time to work on this. I'm already swamped with possibilities and there's stuff I haven't thought of yet. And I haven't really got to grips with the ferry crews yet. Those printouts you got from the ferry manager will require a lot of unscrambling.'

It was a fair answer, especially given the short time Anstruther had been working on the problem.

'Stay with what you're doing,' Smellie said. 'Do you need help?'

'Yes, sir.' A firm reply, with no hint of embarrassment. Smellie wondered if Anstruther knew he was impressing his superiors.

'Speak to Maggie Lampworth, son,' Larch said. 'It might be better to have someone from the county town helping you. She'll have local knowledge. Tall girl, lots of red hair. Tell her I said she was to work with you.'

They sat in silence when Anstruther had gone, then Stewart Pearce rose. 'I'll call the lab about the videos then get the search for the vehicle started.' As the inspector left the room Smellie noted that even after a day in the rain the creases in his trousers were still sharp and wondered how it was done. His own cords were a shapeless mess.

Larch yawned smoke. 'I suppose you guys are going to have a curry or a chinky.'

'Good idea,' Smellie said eagerly. 'The Raj is open on a Sunday.'

'Lucky buggers,' Larch said. 'Me, I have tummy trouble. The wife has to feed me the most awful bloody pap. I'll have a word with the troops then see you in the morning.'

He left, the tiredness showing in his shoulders. Smellie and Naismith looked at each other.

'Are we justified, Bill?'

'I've had half a rotten sausage roll since last night,' Smellie said. 'They owe us an hour.'

They shared a plate of pakora.

'I got the impression you know Stewart Pearce,' Smellie said.

'I met him on a course,' Naismith said. 'He's bright. What I've heard is that he's the brains and Larch is the plodder and they make a good team.'

'So we can leave the vehicle to him. And I trust Anstruther to use his intelligence in finding a connection, with a bit of help. Where does that leave us?'

'Struggling,' Naismith said. 'We need another murder.'

'Don't say that, Jimmy. Sarah says the media are jumping up and down with excitement. They've already given him a name – the Blue Rope Strangler. That's all we need. I hope to hell he doesn't start writing letters to the chief constable or the papers. Or me.'

They stared at each other.

'Remember the Ripper?' Naismith said. 'The hoax tape?'

'I remember. That tape caused the death of several women. I think half the last pakora is mine, thank you very much.'

At Smellie's suggestion, Nalsmith had arranged the meeting in the Ferry Café for ten o'clock on the Monday morning. Behind the counter Theo and Thelma Leaver watched them suspiciously. They appeared to be held together more by grease than mutual affection.

The four women entered and sat down reluctantly. Naismith made the introductions and ordered for everyone.

'Thank you all for coming along,' Smellie said. 'You were friends of Sandra Sim. As you know, she's been murdered and we're desperate to find the killer before he does it again. I'm looking for any kind of information that might give us a lead.'

Silence. The women glanced at each other. Signals were exchanged. The oldest, Joan Liversage, seemed to have been elected spokeswoman.

'We weren't exactly friends, Mr Smellie. We chatted, we had a drink together sometimes, but Sandra always seemed to keep herself to herself, like she wasn't really one of us.'

'Not hoity-toity, like,' another of the women said. Just – different. I don't know.'

'She was on the game because her man was ill,' Joan Liversage said. 'It was like she felt she had a better excuse than the rest of us. Mind you, from what I hear, she kept her old man and the wee boy very smart. Always talking about new curtains and painting the kitchen and like that.'

'What was she like as a person?' Smellie asked, swallowing a mouthful of what had to be the worst cup of tea he had ever tasted.

The women looked at each other again.

'She was OK.'

'Kept herself clean.'

'Businesslike.'

'She had a sharp tongue,' Jane Liversage said. 'Like, she wouldn't take no cheek. She could be pretty sarcastic with anyone that tried to put her down. A bit spiteful, you could say. She wasn't ashamed of what she did or, at least, she never let it show, but you never know.'

'Thank you,' Smellie said. 'Now, can you point us in the direction of anyone you think might have killed her? Did any of you have trouble with a man recently, someone you think may have killed Sandra Sim? Have you heard anything from any of the other ladies that makes you wonder?'

'We've talked about this,' Jane Liversage said. 'We've hardly talked about anything else. If we could think of someone we'd tell you, but we can't.'

She read the expression on Smellie's face. 'Sorry,' she added.

Smellie handed one of his cards to each of them. 'Anything you can think of, anything you learn, however vague, call me. We need your help. He's likely to kill again if we don't catch him, and you ladies are the likeliest targets.'

Naismith was unlocking his car door when Smellie's mobile sounded.

'It's Stewart Pearce, sir, at HQ. Robbie's on his way to see you and I'll be right behind him. He's had a letter from the strangler.'

5

'It's a photocopy,' Larch said. 'Probably a photocopy of a photocopy, to make things difficult for the lab. Posted in the box outside the main post office in Brickhill some time on Sunday. He addressed it to me at Police HQ and marked it URGENT – MURDER! and it was delivered first thing. Brown business envelope, first class stamp. The lab will check for anything useful but something tells me he knew better than to give us a sample of his saliva.'

Smellie read the photocopy. The original had been printed in boxy capital letters on lined paper with a margin and holes ready punched for filing.

HELLO, ROBBIE.

THE KILLING OF KAREN POTTER WAS NOT A ONE-OFF. SHE WAS JUST THE FIRST OF MANY. SANDRA SIM WAS THE SECOND. THEY TAKE YOUR MONEY BUT DON'T GIVE ANYTHING IN RETURN AND YOU CAN HEAR THEM LAUGHING AT YOU BEHIND YOUR BACK AFTERWARDS. WELL, I'M GOING TO PUNISH THEM ALL, ONE BY ONE, UNTIL THEY'RE ALL DEAD AND DECENT PEOPLE WILL THANK ME. YOU'RE A POLICEMAN, ROBBIE, SO YOU KNOW AS WELL AS I DO THE DIFFERENCE BETWEEN GOOD AND EVIL. I KNOW YOU HAVE YOUR JOB TO DO, BUT DON'T YOU SECRETLY, IN YOUR HEART OF HEARTS, APPLAUD WHAT I'M DOING? THEY ARE MARKED WITH THE SIGN OF

THE DEVIL AND MUST BE PUNISHED. I SEE YOU'RE NOT SAYING ANYTHING ABOUT THE PANTIES AND THE POUND. THEY'LL BE OUR SECRET SO YOU'LL ALWAYS KNOW IT'S ME.

Smellie passed the letter to Naismith. 'Obviously not a hoax, unless our security is suspect and word about the panties and the coin has got out. And he's threatening to kill again.'

Larch nodded. 'That's the bit makes me sick to my stomach.'

'Has Stewart come up with anything on the vehicle?'

Larch brought the giant pipe from his pocket and Smellie glanced at the windows. He had opened them before Larch arrived.

'The lab people have been working on the videos, but all they can say is that it's a Series 3 Land Rover 110 van, number not visible. There's a possibility the number plate may have been obscured with mud or something like that. They've had people from Rover look at the videos, but Rover have built thousands of these vehicles, especially the green ones, and the design's remained the same for years. We won't get any further from the video. And I've had people go through the CCTV videos from the first murder yet again but the eight Land Rovers they saw were all short wheelbase, or long wheelbase estates, or clearly a different colour.'

Smellie sat back in his chair. 'The Land Rover is our only hope, Robbie. It's not absolutely certain the killer of Sandra Sim was driving that vehicle, but it's the only lead we have. I talked to Anstruther and Lampworth this morning and they're just getting bogged down in connections. Anstruther reckons our likeliest bet is a birdwatcher who likes whist drives and pub quizzes and is looking for a second-hand car at an auction.'

There was no hint of humour in Larch's face. 'Are they following that up?'

It seemed pointless to mention that Anstruther had been exaggerating for effect. 'I left it with them.'

'Doesn't seem likely,' Larch muttered. 'We're grinding down, Bill. We've reached that stage where we have a mass of information which is no bloody use and we don't know where to go next.'

'How about going public with the Land Rover?' Naismith said. 'Ask for any information.'

'We're holding on that for the moment,' Larch said. 'We can do that when we've completed our own check. We'll be issuing a press release later today asking for witnesses to either crime. There's no shortage of media coverage, as you've probably noticed: I can't show my face in public without them sticking microphones down my throat, and the chief constable's getting a lot of flak from the MPs and the Press and that's working its way down to me.'

There was a knock on the door and Stewart Pearce entered and sat opposite Smellie. Today he had chosen a checked tweed suit and brown brogues and a striped tie. He made Smellie feel dowdy.

'An update, sir, on the vehicle. I've had sixty-one officers working on this, but they're not finished yet. So far they've managed to eliminate about a third of the Land Rovers on the list. The picture is complicated by the fact that there are a lot of Land Rovers in the county which are registered elsewhere, and a lot of the Land Rovers registered here are now scattered all over the country.'

'Do you have any suspicions, Stewart?' Larch asked.

'We've found people we may want to talk to again. One hundred and forty-eight people cannot provide proof that they were not at the location of one or both of the murders. That's assuming we refuse to accept alibis without witnesses. There are tales of vehicles being bogged down in mud, or waiting for a spare part, or on loan, and there's the usual proportion who can't remember where they were on a Saturday night a month ago. I instructed all officers to examine the vehicles and be on the lookout for blue rope. They found forty-six vehicles with blue rope in them or nearby. Just about everyone who has a boat of any kind uses blue polypropylene rope, and people with boats often have Land Rovers to tow them around and drag them out of the water. And farmers use the stuff a lot, and so do tradesmen, and anyone with a roof rack or a trailer. I get the impression people who drive Land Rovers are forever tying things to them, usually with blue polypropylene rope.'

'So where are you?' Larch asked.

'Collecting information, collating it, ready to start looking for connections once we get more information. There's nobody standing out as a prime suspect. The registration number would solve everything. The lab has established that one of the ends of the blue rope was cut using snips like you find in DIY supermarkets.'

Silence fell. They all understood the enormity of the problem.

'A third murder would give us more statistics to work on,' Pearce said. 'Two murders just leave us with a lot of loose ends. We're still working on the problem, but it will be the weekend before we've spoken to everyone. And there's always the chance the man we want to speak to has taken off, or gave a false name originally, or never notified Swansea about the change of ownership of the vehicle, or is from outside the area, or whatever.'

'It's odd that he brought the Land Rover right to the scene of the crime,' Smellie said. 'You'd think he'd park round the corner at least, or better still a couple of streets away. If the Land Rover is actually connected to the killing, that is; the driver may just have stopped for a fish supper or a cup of tea in the café and we're just wasting hundreds of hours of police time.'

'It was raining,' Larch said. 'And, going by the letter, he's a cocky bugger. Overconfident. Maybe he just preferred to have the vehicle handy for a quick getaway. Maybe he was just cruising and spotted Sandra Sim and stopped. Or maybe, as you say, the Land Rover's got nothing to do with it and we're farting up a drainpipe. But we've got to keep looking.'

Smellie answered the phone. 'Send her in.' He replaced the receiver and looked at Larch. 'The Forensic psychologist has arrived.'

Sarah Noonan knocked and opened the door of Smellie's office. 'Dr Peabody, sir.'

Smellie rose. 'Thank you. Come in, Doctor. Sit down, please. Can I get you coffee?'

'Love that.'

Smellie nodded to Sarah, recognizing the amusement in her dark eyes. Dr Peabody was not what they had been expecting. Dr Peabody was in her twenties and about five feet high in her yellow suede boots; somehow the bounce of ash-blonde hair and the cornflower blue eyes behind the granny specs gave her enough femininity to carry off the army surplus DPM jacket and faded blue jeans.

She hefted a briefcase on to Smellie's desk and plumped herself down in a chair and showed large white teeth in a smile.

'Am I late? I came by train and it seemed to take forever.'

'No problem,' Smellie said and made the introductions.

'Well, Doctor,' Larch said, 'have you anything for us? Have you worked out a psychological profile of the killer?' It was clear from his voice that he had no great hopes of Dr Peabody.

'Yes. But before I start, have you anything new for me, any additional information?'

'There's this,' Smellie said, sliding the photocopied letter across the desk. 'It arrived this morning and everything indicates it's not a hoax. There are details in it which are not in the public domain.'

'Thank you. Give me a minute.'

She examined the letter minutely and read it several times. If she's faking her self-confidence, Smellie thought, she's making a very good job of it. He watched her rake around in her briefcase, find a grid printed on clear plastic and lay it over the photocopy and examine it closely for some time, making notes on a reporter's pad. Larch shifted impatiently in his chair and stared out the window. It was fully ten minutes before Dr Peabody put the letter aside and took out a file and looked round their faces.

'You're satisfied the letter's for real?'

'The bit about the panties and the pound coin is being kept secret,' Smellie said. 'There's nothing to indicate this information has leaked out. Keep it that way.'

'Good.' Dr Peabody opened the file. 'The printing is faked, of course: the same letters are quite different in different parts of the document. I suppose you spotted that. But the spacing and alignment are consistent and the grammar and spelling are spot-on and the meaning perfectly clear, so we're dealing with someone who is educated. Have you sent it to a graphologist?'

'Yes.'

'Right. I'd like to see the report. The content is interesting. A hint of paranoia, a hint of religious mania, a hint of self-righteousness, a hint of arrogance. All of which ties in quite well with what we worked out from the information you supplied. I should say I worked on your report with Professor Hendrikson; he's tied up at the moment, but he and I are agreed on the analysis and I'll be getting back to him with this new information.'

'So who are we looking for?' Larch asked. He sounded like a man who had doubts.

Dr Peabody turned a page in the file. 'Out of all the information you supplied, there were just a few points we could work on. The absence of sex, the panties, the pound coin, the method of killing, the appearance of the two women, the vehicle. The fact that there was no sex and that the panties were removed often indicates an inability to perform when the occasion demands. The individual feels more confident working alone, with the panties for stimulation. It's a common enough problem, one which the individual frequently tries to overcome when young then accepts and adapts to and may eventually come to prefer, but it's also a situation which can create deep-seated anger. The individual blames women for this condition, and frequently one woman in particular, someone he knew when he was young, someone who robbed him of his self-confidence at a crucial moment and probably laughed at him because he failed. In this case, very probably, a slim woman with dark hair and black stockings, like the dead women.'

Dr Peabody took a mouthful of coffee and made a face, 'Cold. Could I have another cup?'

Smellie used the phone to order five coffees. 'Go on, please.'

'We're into revenge now,' Dr Peabody said. 'Self-righteous hatred seemingly associated with religion – the references to the Devil and punishment. The individual refuses to accept that he is in any way at fault, however innocently, and blames the women. He chooses to see himself as an avenger appointed by God to eliminate evil women linked to the Devil.'

In any other company, Smellie thought, stuff like this would be rejected as fanciful. But we're policemen and we've met some weird people and we're not surprised.

'What about the pound coin in the mouth?'

'A symbol,' Dr Peabody said. 'All women are prostitutes, selling their bodies for profit. But really, of course, what he's saying is, that girl I knew when I was young ruined everything for me and it's her I'm punishing and I want everyone to know she was nothing better than a prostitute, however proper and respectable she was and however respectably married she may be now.'

Coffee was delivered and there was a break while they all sugared and stirred and added milk.

'You mentioned the Land Rover,' Pearce said. 'What does that mean?'

'Nothing psychological. Just that no one buys and drives a long wheelbase Land Rover van from choice. It's one of those vehicles you drive because you have a job or a business that requires that kind of vehicle.'

'So?'

'So it suggests a small businessman or someone working for a firm which allows the driver to use the vehicle after hours. It may mean that the driver can't afford a vehicle of his own, or that the driver runs a rather unsuccessful small business. Or that he's a farmer, I suppose.'

'What about the rope?' Naismith asked. 'The choice of weapon.'

'You can look at that various ways,' Dr Peabody said. 'There may be perfectly straightforward reasons for that choice of instrument: availability; the absence of other weapons; to ensure silence; to avoid bloodstains on the murderer's clothing. Or it may have a symbolic significance. Strangulation is a form of hanging, which is official execution, or used to be. That would tie in with what he hints at in his letter about acting like judge, jury and executioner, with public approval.'

They all stared at her. 'Could you summarize, please,' Smellie said. 'Who are we looking for?'

Dr Peabody smiled. 'They all ask that, and they've every right to do so. After all, it's supposed to be my job. But I'm struggling from lack of information. Another murder would be useful. However. . . .'

She drew a page from the file and laid it on the desk.

'You'll appreciate that we're working from a bare minimum of information. All we've been able to do is look at similar cases, averages, precedents. If you were to come up with one new or different fact it could change the whole picture.'

'Understood,' Larch said impatiently.

'Very well. This is all speculative. We're trying to give you something to work on, but we could be misleading you. I have to say that. OK. Age: possible upper limit thirty-five, because in many people personality disorders seem to mature at about that time and the individual learns to cope, or perhaps takes on responsibilities like a wife and children, or just loses steam. But maybe it took your man longer to reach that stage, so he could be older. Family background: very probably unsatisfactory. A broken home or a violent parent or foster parents or an institution. Probably a religious element in the upbringing, but not in the good sense of the word. He may have a small penis. Professor Hendrikson and I had assumed a poor level of education, because that's the norm in cases similar to this one, but the letter disproves that. As I said, one extra fact can change everything. We had combined the Land Rover van with our guess at a poor education and come up with the likelihood of a menial job, but that's scrubbed now. Probably a loner, even if he takes part in social activities. Acquaintances, perhaps, but no close friends. He's not likely to be very good company.'

She looked round the intent faces.

'We've pencilled him in as someone with a psychopathic personality, which means someone who has not been able to develop a normal moral sense. He has killed twice and he has probably achieved sexual gratification as a result. He's probably been thinking of all this for years and now he's done it successfully and he's sure of himself and he'll be wanting to do it again. It will make him feel good about himself, which may be a new sensation for him.'

She tapped the photocopied letter.

'A need to boast is quite common in this condition. Whether he knows it or not, sending you this letter is boasting. That's a broad outline, based on limited information. Please don't let all this blind you to the possibility that the man you're looking for is quite different. Let me know if you learn anything new and we'll try to be more precise.'

'Where did all that get us, Bill?' Larch asked, as they paused in the front hall of Divisional HQ.

'Nowhere,' Smellie said. 'There's nothing in what she said that we can use safely. The description's too vague to be useful. Except, perhaps, the bit about the vehicle, and that may be a blind alley. What are you going to do now?'

'Get back to HQ and see what's been happening. There's a press conference set for two o'clock and Fowler wants to see me before then. I have a feeling he may want to take over the investigation personally.'

Smellie had been anticipating the same thing. 'That wouldn't imply criticism of us, Robbie.'

Larch touched Smellie's elbow. 'Very tactfully put, son.'

6

The Harbour Bar was empty except for two men and a woman at a corner table. The man behind the counter was short and fat with a red face and no apparent faith in antiperspirants.

'He's clocked us already,' Naismith murmured as he and Smellie took stools at the end of the bar. 'Don't risk the beer. Guaranteed laxative.'

'Yes, gentlemen?'

'Two Grouse,' Smellie said. 'It's Harvey Nolan, isn't it?' He avoided the sight of Nolan's wet armpit as the publican reached up to the gantry.

'That's right. It's Mr Smellie and Mr Naismith, isn't it? You'll be working on the murder of Sandra Sim. Two of your blokes were in earlier.'

'Correct,' Smellie said. 'I've read their report. You weren't very helpful.'

Nolan looked offended. 'Told them all I could, Mr Smellie, sir. Anxious to help. Wasn't much, but it was all I had.'

Sly and Driver had talked to Harvey Nolan; they were both large men and could appear threatening, which sometimes produced the wrong response. Smellie added a little water to the two glasses.

'We're not here to hassle you, Mr Nolan. This is a murder

enquiry and we need your help. Any scrap of information you can give us. The sooner we get this guy the sooner the other ladies will be safe, including your friend Avril Willingshaw. We don't really care if some of the ladies work from your pub, and for the moment we don't really care that drugs are sold in your pub.'

That had been a guess, but it was obvious from Nolan's face that the guess had been correct.

'Help us find this guy, Mr Nolan. Anything you can give us, even if it doesn't make much sense to you. Do any of your customers drive a Land Rover?'

Nolan poured himself a dark rum and sank half of it. 'There's a bloke comes in sometimes, drives a BT Land Rover.'

'No good.'

'There's a bloke parks his Land Rover across the road a lot of the time, but he doesn't come in.'

'What type of Land Rover?'

'One with windows at the back. Estate, sort of. Can't think of anyone else.'

Smellie knew of the Land Rover in question; the owner had already been checked out. 'All right. Now, what about Sandra Sim? Was she a regular?'

'Most nights, when she was working. In and out two or three times between eight o'clock and closing.'

'Did she have customers among your regulars? I know what you told my officers, but I'd like you to think again.'

'I don't like—'

'Mr Nolan, I really don't care what you don't like. I want answers.'

Nolan read the expression on Smellie's face and dropped his eyes to his glass.

'There are one or two. They come here knowing they'll find the ladies.'

'Names and addresses, descriptions, the nights they come in, the vehicles they drive, everything you can give us. Concentrate on Saturday night.'

Naismith wrote busily in his notebook while the publican stumbled through a brief account.

'That's all I know, Mr Smellie. Some names, no addresses, one car. Someone walks in, I don't ask for identification. And, after dark, I've no idea what's happening in the street, unless I go to the door, so I don't know what people are driving.'

'Understood. Thank you. Now, anyone you wondered about? Maybe someone who came in and watched the ladies but didn't approach them? Especially last Saturday night.'

'Can't think of anyone last Saturday. That's our busiest night of the week, and it's pretty frantic.'

'Try hard. You know your regulars. Tell us about the ones you don't know. Maybe a guy on his own in a hat with the brim turned down and a long anorak or a short coat.'

Harvey Nolan refreshed their glasses. 'On the house. There were people I didn't know last Saturday, but I can't remember anyone alone.' He looked round the pub, eyes squinting, remembering. 'Couple over there, both on cider; they left early. Four young lads at the table there, lager, made a bit of noise, drank more than they were capable of, probably threw up before they got to the chinky. Sandra and Avril were beside the bandit, like always, chatting to anyone that passed. Vodka and bitter lemon for Sandra, gin and tonic for Avril. The usual crowd at the bar. It was raining, so everyone had coats or anoraks or like that.' He shook his head. 'Sorry, Mr Smellie, but I don't remember anyone I'd point a finger at. And I am trying to help.'

'When Sandra Sim left for the last time and didn't come back, did anyone go out immediately after her, as if he were following?'

Nolan stared at the door, frowning. 'I think I'd have noticed, but no, I don't think so.'

Smellie emptied his glass and dropped one of his cards on the bar.

'Anything you think of or remember, call me. Thanks for your help.'

They walked back to Smellie's car. The rain had stopped and a strong wind coming off the moors suggested there might be a change in the weather at last.

'That didn't help much,' Naismith said.

'It helped a little. Landlords always have a very good idea what's happening in their pubs. They don't miss much. If Harvey Nolan reckons our man didn't latch on to Sandra Sim in the Harbour Bar then he's probably correct, which brings us right back to the guy who may or may not have arrived in a Land Rover.'

'We need to saturate the area on Saturday, Bill,' Naismith said. 'See what's going on. Talk to the Saturday night crowd. Show them Sandra Sim's photograph, maybe show them a mock-up of the strangler.'

Smellie nodded. 'We'll do that. Start planning ahead: everyone on duty and fully briefed, everyone with a specific area to cover. I'll talk to the super about getting some extra bodies. And we still have other work to be done and people appearing in court. Put Sarah on to that. Tell her she has full authority to bend the rules any way she wants.'

'OK.'

'He's going to do it again, Jimmy, and he'll go on doing it until we stop him. So let's get the bastard.'

Naismith raised an eyebrow. It was rare for William Smellie to resort to coarse language.

The big man sat at the table in the interview room and scraped out his pipe into the ashtray. He had already been interviewed for three hours by Grossmith and Driver when Smellie entered.

'Right, Mr Fairman, let's go through it again.'

'Look, mister—'

'We'll go through it again!'

They glared at each other. Fairman broke first.

'If you want.'

'You drive an artic,' Smellie said. 'You're a regular customer with Sandra Sim. You've admitted that. When was the last time?'

'I've already been through that. . . .'

'Tell me again!'

'Last Saturday.'

'That was the night she was murdered.'

'I didn't kill her, mister. I've told the other guys. . . .'

'I know what you've told my officers. That's why I'm here. You met Sandra Sim late on Saturday evening. She was murdered late on Saturday evening. When exactly did you meet her?'

'I've said, I'm not sure. Some time before eleven o'clock. At the café.'

'Inside or outside?'

'Inside.'

'Go on.'

'So we done it.'

'You left the café with Sandra Sim. We have a witness to that. Go on from there.'

'I'm parked along the street. We get in the cab and we have it off. I've got a bunk behind the cab. She liked it back there.'

'Where were you parked?'

'Across from the chip shop.'

'Witnesses?'

'I don't know.'

'A witness would help you, Mr Fairman.'

'You find a bloody witness! That's your job, innit?'

'Don't raise your voice to me!'

'Sorry.'

'What proof do you have of what you're telling me?'

The big man shrugged. 'I gave her four new fivers, straight out my pay packet. Apart from that, I dunno.'

There had been four new five-pound notes with consecutive numbers in Sandra Sim's purse. The numbers would be checked against the notes supplied to Andrew Fairman's employers by the bank.

'Did you see a Land Rover parked on Shore Street or in the neighbourhood?'

'No.'

'That's all for the moment, Mr Fairman. We may need to talk to you again. You can go.'

'Thank Christ for that.'

When he had gone, Smellie nodded to Grossmith. 'Check the money with the bank. Who else do we have?'

'Maxwell Thornton, age thirty-five, schoolteacher. Married, no children, wife also a schoolteacher, father a headmaster, mother-in-law assistant director of education with the council. He's shitting himself. He took Sandra Sim round the huts some time between half ten and eleven o'clock on Saturday night. His attitude seems to be, if we can't prove anything then it didn't happen.'

'Wheel him in.'

Sarah Noonan moved her head a fraction to attract Smellie's attention as he walked into the incident room.

'Call from Mr Fowler. Call back.'

'Smellie went to his office and tapped out the number, already guessing what he was about to hear from Chief Detective Inspector Norman Fowler.

'Smellie, the chief constable has put me in charge of the investigation into these two murders. No reflection on you and

Robbie Larch, but it looks like we have a serious problem here and he feels we should go straight to a full-scale effort immediately. I want the top two investigating officers from every division at HQ at eight o'clock tonight for a conference.'

Smellie drew up outside Naismith's semi and tapped the horn and watched his friend come down the path and get into the car.

'I hate getting dressed up,' Naismith said.

'I didn't realize you had.'

'Bog off.'

Four hours later Smellie drew up outside Naismith's house for the second time that evening.

'Coffee?'

'I'd rather have coffee with a young lady,' Smellie said.

'Mmm. Be like that.'

Smellie grinned. 'See you in the morning, sweetie.'

Jane Grey was ready for bed, the white towelling robe tied over some kind of short nightie. She made no attempt to avoid Smellie's grasp.

'So what do you want, apart from the obvious?'

'I'm hungry. The Raj is still open.'

'I'm not going to get dressed again. I'll make you something. How long are you going to be here?' She had learned long since that she had no proprietary rights over Smellie's time.

'All night,' Smellie said. 'But an early start.'

'That's good enough. Let's have a look in the fridge. Get me a drink.'

Even with her face shiny and her hair tousled she looks good enough to eat, Smellie thought. And she knows it, because she's making no attempt to rush to her bedroom to tart herself up. She has self-confidence and I like that. What the hell does she see in me?

He prepared two iced gins with tonic and a splash of lemon juice and took them through to the kitchen. Jane was cutting chicken fillets into strips.

'Cheers. Do some rice, lover.'

'What is it?'

'Stir-fried chicken with. . .' She checked the vegetable rack and opened a cupboard door. 'Stir-fried chicken with a red pepper and a chilli and some shallots and soy sauce and dry mustard and sesame oil and olive oil and garlic. And anything else I happen to come across.'

'Sounds great.'

'I called you this evening and they said you were at a conference at HQ.'

Smellie rinsed the rice. 'Fowler's been put in charge of the investigation. It is now officially a hunt for a serial killer.'

'The Blue Rope Strangler. He's getting a lot of airtime on the TV news.'

'Uh-huh. We're going to throw everything we have into the investigation. Every officer not absolutely essential to other work will be involved.'

'Which means?'

'Which means we don't know nothing. It's very difficult to pinpoint someone you don't know anything about. Fowler summarized the evidence so far and when you come right down to it the only thing we know for certain is that he used a bit of blue rope. All the rest is circumstantial. He may be driving a Land Rover van, but that's not certain. He may be a religious psychopath, but that may be a clever cover-up. He may have a small prick and a down on slim women with long dark hair, but maybe that's a false trail. He may hate prostitutes and he may get his jollies from women's panties, but maybe not. There was a month between the two murders, so maybe he's affected by the phases of the moon, or maybe not.'

Jane stirred the sizzling chicken. 'Maybe it's a woman suffering from pre-menstrual tension.'

Smellie stared at her. 'I suggested something like that but I was laughed out of court.'

'You need another murder.'

'Everyone keeps saying that. We don't want another murder.'

'I know, but you'd get more information.'

Smellie dropped a parsley and garlic stock cube into the rice pot. 'We might not learn anything new and there would be another dead woman.'

'So what are you working on?'

'The sighting of a Land Rover, which may or may not be relevant. There are hundreds of the damn' things in the county, but it's the only lead we have and we're pushing it hard. And every available officer will be on the ground every Saturday night from now on.'

Jane added the chopped pepper and some of the chilli and the halved shallots. 'What if he kills again on a Tuesday?'

'We'll look stupid. We're advised these people tend to stick to a pattern, but I'm not sure, myself.'

He watched her crush two cloves of garlic and stir them into the wok. The smell was mouth-watering. The rice was coming to the boil and he turned the gas down and stirred gently then replaced the lid.

'Red?'

'It's all there is. That bottle of Serret you brought last week is still there. Why the four-week interval?'

'That's what's puzzling us,' Smellie said. 'We have five officers working on that full-time, trying to spot a pattern, a connection, any reason for our man being in two places at the same time on the same day of the week four weeks apart. Remember DC Anstruther?'

'Tall, spotty and eager?'

'That's the fella. He's been working twenty hours a day on this, and he's been given four DCs to assist him. I spotted him kissing one of them in a dark corner this evening.'

'Heavens above!'

'It's all right, it was Maggie Lampworth. She wasn't unhappy about it. And she's quite attractive, in an Arnold Schwarzenegger sort of way.'

'I'm so glad. Has he discovered anything?'

Smellie drew the cork. 'The social, leisure and religious life of the county. I suppose, when you come down to it, everyone does something in their spare time. Strange things. Accountants go paint-balling. Doctors go line dancing. Bricklayers go fossilling. Florists pump iron. Vicars have black belts in the martial arts. Music teachers go rock climbing. Club bouncers paint water-colours. And when you permutate their activities trying to find reasons for one strangler to be in two places four weeks apart in a Land Rover you vanish under a heap of information. Poor Anstruther is going quietly mad.'

'And how many of them hate slim women with long dark hair?'

'Unknown quantity. More soy sauce.' He poured two glasses of wine then set a kettle to boil for rinsing the rice.

'That was good,' Smellie said, laying his plate on the coffee table and picking up his glass. 'Better than good. Delicious.'

'Thank you. The rice was perfect, as usual.'

'I know. Any more?'

'All gone.'

'Want to make love?'

'Of course.' Jane Grey smiled. 'I've a feeling I'd better grab you while you're available. You have the air of a man who may very well be tied up for some time to come.'

'Many a true word spoken in a vest.'

She moved along the couch and he slipped an arm round her shoulders and drew her close.

'Why do you put up with me?' he asked.

'You have warm hands.'

'Is that all?'

'There's a certain thrill about your irregularity. I think I'm faced with another night alone and suddenly you're there, panting with lust or more likely just hungry, and it's very exciting. Stir fried chicken and red wine at midnight, the threat that you'll have to leave suddenly. Spontaneity. Urgency. It turns a lady on.'

'Are you deliberately showing your legs?'

'Yes.'

'You have gorgeous legs.'

'I know. And I know you like them. They're my contribution to the gaiety of nations.'

'Slut.'

'Whatever you say, lover.'

Smellie woke from a deep sleep and stared uncomprehendingly in the direction of the phone ringing on the bedside cabinet. The fluorescent hands of Jane Grey's alarm showed 4.37 but it was difficult to work out if that meant morning or evening.

'Smellie.'

'Barry, sir. Sorry to disturb you, but the desk just took a call from a Mr Elliot Samson. He says he's spotted a body in a ditch up on the moors, about five miles out on the road to Kingsfoot. A woman. He says there's a blue rope round her neck.'

7

There was already a patrol car on site when Smellie arrived. The two officers had left the headlights on and were standing in the glare looking down into the ditch. A white Volvo was parked nearby, a figure leaning against the door smoking a cigarette.

'Detective Superintendent Smellie, Garrmouth Division. Mr Samson?'

The grey-haired man nodded. 'Yes. I phoned in on the mobile. I saw a foot sticking out of the grass and stopped and found a woman lying over there. Look, I've given my name and address and car number and explained that I have a plane to catch. I'll be in deep shit if I'm not in Amsterdam when I'm expected.'

'Off you go, Mr Samson. Thank you for your help.'

The Volvo left at speed. Smellie walked down the road and introduced himself to PCs Patterson and Imrie.

'What have you done?'

'I checked she wasn't still alive, sir,' Patterson said. 'I'm no expert, but she's cold and there's a blue rope round her neck and no sign of life.'

He exhaled noisily into the glare of the headlights; in the chill of the night his breath showed clearly. 'Didn't see any breath, sir.'

'All right. Lend me your torch.'

The body was lying on its back in a grassy ditch about three feet below the level of the unfenced road. One leg had been caught up on a tussock and the foot pointed oddly skywards. Smellie learned what he could without disturbing the grass further.

'One of you, take your car up the road then turn and come back and try to see what Mr Samson saw. Assume he was moving quite fast. We'll have the torches out while you do that.'

A few minutes later PC Imrie switched off the engine of the patrol car and returned. 'The foot's quite obvious, sir. Showed up in the headlights.'

'Thank you.' Smellie watched lights approaching. 'Do you have tape with you?'

'Yes, sir.'

'Well, get the site taped off, please. Give it plenty of room. Watch where you're putting your feet. In particular, don't damage any tyre tracks.'

Dawn revealed a clear sky with small white clouds chased by a bitter wind and a dozen vehicles parked along the single-track road. From here, in a hollow in the moors, there was no view of the sea. Smellie stood in the shelter of one of the Scene of Crime vans and shivered. The waxed cotton coat over a suit was inadequate protection against the cold.

'I'm going to have to leave some warm clothing at Jane's place,' he muttered. 'I keep getting caught out.'

'Get yourself a nice warm anorak,' Naismith said. He looked perfectly at ease, a red woolly hat pulled down over his ears, the swarthy face apparently immune to the wind.

Chief Detective Inspector Fowler and Detective Superintendent Larch watched the body being removed to an ambulance and the white-overalled figures of Scene of Crime moving into inspect the flattened grass. Smellie and Naismith joined them.

'Anything useful, sir?' Smellie asked.

'Just the tyre print,' Fowler said. 'Everything indicates she was killed somewhere else and dumped here.' His belly strained the front of his raincoat and he clamped a hand on the blue felt hat to stop it being blown off. His smart black shoes were marked by damp and mud and he looked cold.

'We know her name,' Larch said, 'from a couple of credit cards in her purse in her pocket. Mrs Laura Beale. We'll soon track her down. Obviously another working girl, although she looks a bit older than the average. Blue rope, like the others, and there was a pound coin under her tongue. It looks as if he tried to take her panties, but she was wearing tights instead of stockings and he gave up. But they're halfway down and torn.'

'She may not be a working girl,' Smellie said. 'Her clothes and shoes were expensive and she was wearing tights and the pendant round her neck and the rings are valuable. And there's a George Beale who is the manager at the ferry terminal. There's a possibility the strangler has made a mistake.'

Everyone stared at him. Fowler spoke first. 'Has this George Beale reported his wife missing?'

'Not so far as I know, sir.'

'Well, check on that, Smellie. Don't keep us in suspense. But in the meantime we'll have the office run a search for other women with the same name.'

The detached house in Park Crescent had a double garage and a security light and a monobloc driveway. The garden was meticulous rather than inspired. Worth about £175,000 by now, Smellie decided, but probably bought new for less than £10,000. There was a light on in the hall.

George Beale answered the door in shirt and tie and neatly pressed suit trousers. He touched his mouth with a napkin.

'Hello, Mr Smellie.'

'Good morning, sir. May we come in?'

'Of course. You're early on the job.'

Smellie entered the house, Naismith following. There was a smell of furniture polish and coffee. Beale looked at them expectantly.

'Could I have a word with your wife, please, sir.'

Beale stared at him. 'I doubt if she has anything useful to say about the murder of that woman, Mr Smellie. If that's what you're here about.'

'Is she awake, sir?'

'Should be, by now, though she had a late night.'

Beale went upstairs. Smellie and Naismith looked around. A marmalade cat appeared at the kitchen door and stared at them then vanished. The pictures on the walls were middle-of-the-road water-colours, but all originals. An open door revealed a comfortable sitting-room with a large television set and a leather three-piece suite. A barometer hung on one wall.

George Beale appeared at the top of the stairs, his face suddenly alert.

'Why are you here, Mr Smellie?'

'Mrs Beale?'

'She doesn't appear to be here.' Beale came down the stairs slowly, one hand gripping the banister. 'Why isn't she here? I've checked the spare rooms as well.'

'When did you see her last, sir?'

Beale stopped on the half-landing, frowning. 'I dropped her off at the Marine Hotel at about nine o'clock last night. She's a member of a keep-fit class and they were having a mid-session pub supper. They have a drink so she didn't want to drive.'

'And when did she get home, sir?'

George Beale twisted the napkin in his hands as he descended the stairs.

'I don't know. She was going to walk home or get a taxi, because she didn't know when they'd be finished. It's only a ten-minute walk. We sleep in different rooms, you see, because I snore. I went to bed at the usual time and fell asleep.'

He looked at Smellie and Naismith, the uncertainty showing on his face. 'Maybe she stayed with one of her friends. But you're here, so. . . .'

'Do you have a photograph of your wife, sir?'

'Yes. Where?' Beale frowned and shook his head. 'Yes, of course, through here.'

He led them into the kitchen and pointed to a row of photographs stacked against plates on a Dutch dresser. 'That's Laura with our grandchild.'

Smellie and Naismith stared at the pictures. They showed an attractive woman, slim and dark-haired, in various poses with an infant.

'That's Marie, our first grandchild,' Beale said. He swallowed audibly. 'Now, please tell me why you're here. Has something happened?'

Smellie sighed. 'Mr Beale, a woman has been found dead up on the moors. I'm afraid it may be your wife.'

George Beale raised a hand and touched the front of Smellie's coat then sank to his knees and collapsed in a heap.

The manager of the Marine Hotel was a lanky man with soft fair hair. He listened to Smellie and shook his head in disbelief.

'Come into my office, please,' he whispered. 'I'll find my wife and get her to join you.'

Smellie and DC Marianne Cross sat down and waited in silence. The door opened and a plump woman of about forty bustled in. Smellie rose.

'I'm Kitty Richards,' the woman said. 'What's this about Laura? Is she really *dead*?'

'I'm afraid so, Mrs Richards. Mr Beale has formally identified the body. It was not an accident.'

She slumped into the chair behind the desk. 'This is horrible. She was here last night, and she was so *alive*, so full of *life*, so *happy*.' She opened a drawer and found a box of tissues and dabbed carefully at her eyes. Smellie guessed she put a good deal of effort into her appearance. The intricate crown of auburn hair looked set in concrete.

'We need to know about her movements last night, Mrs Richards,' he said, sitting down. 'When she left here, who she left with, was she on foot or did she get a lift or take a taxi. Everything you can tell us, please.'

'We had such a lovely evening. The keep fit class. We meet twice a week at the civic centre and once every session we have an evening. We had the Oak Room.' Mrs Richards sighed. 'It's just a few drinks and a buffet, really, but we have such a *lovely* time. Jaqui had done a video of one of our classes and we fell about when we saw it. And we all *cheered* Laura; she's the best of all of us on the mini-trampoline. We called her the bouncing beauty. And we talked, of course, the way women do.'

'When did you finish up?' Smellie asked. Cross had her note-book and pen ready, but Kitty Richards still hadn't said anything worth noting.

'It was after eleven. It's *amazing* how the time passes. Well after eleven. More like half past.'

'Can you be precise, Mrs Richards?'

The snub nose was blown daintily. 'Say about twenty past eleven, although it didn't all happen at once. It probably took about ten minutes in all for everyone to get their coats and say goodnight and so on. Some of the girls had to call their husbands to come and collect them, and there was the usual congregation in the lobby. I can't remember if Laura was waiting for George, but probably not. There was a bit of a joke about . . . you know.'

'About what?'

Kitty Richards actually blushed. 'About fifteen fit ladies with a drink in them going home to terrified husbands. But I remember Laura saying George would probably be sound asleep by the time she got in. He has an early start in the morning.'

'So did she walk or take a taxi or get a lift?'

'I don't know. She and Pat Lowndes went out the door together; I remember that bit.'

Patricia Lowndes was the sole owner of the Pine Shop in the High Street. She was a tall, angular woman in her fifties, severely unattractive to Smellie's eye. She displayed anger rather than tears when he explained why he was there.

'You don't seem to be making much of a job of protecting the citizens, Mr Smellie. Two murders a week is a bit much. Was she strangled?'

'Yes, I'm afraid she was. I need to know what she did and where she went after she left the Marine last night. Mrs Richards is of the opinion you and Mrs Beale left together.'

'That's right.'

'Go on, please.'

'Well, we walked up Palmerston Place to the High Street and stood chatting for a minute or two, then I came home – I live upstairs, above the shop – and Laura went off across the High Street towards Park Crescent.'

'So she was walking home.'

'Of course. She had only another five minutes walk to go when she left me.'

Smellie stared at the pale-blue eyes and aggressive nose and decided that Patricia Lowndes was a practical woman.

'Everything indicates that Laura Beale never reached home,

Ms Lowndes. Somewhere between leaving you and getting home she met someone and was probably enticed or forced into a vehicle and transported to a spot five miles up on to the moors and dumped in a ditch. By that time she was dead. Can you help me? Did you see anything suspicious? Any vehicle parked in the vicinity? Any vehicle following you up Palmerston Place? A man standing around, or following you on foot?'

Patricia Lowndes stared out through the big window at the passing traffic and frowned.

'There were vehicles. The street wasn't busy. There were parked cars.' She shook her head impatiently. 'Dammit, we don't use our eyes, do we? I'm sorry, but I can't remember seeing anything that jumped out at me. Nothing that made me think, that's odd. Nothing that made me think maybe Laura shouldn't be walking home alone.'

'Did you see a Land Rover?'

'I don't think so.'

'Let's walk.'

'Where, sir?' Cross asked.

'Up Park Crescent from the corner of the High Street and Palmerston Place.'

'The route taken by the murdered woman.'

'Yes.'

They stood at the corner for a minute then crossed the High Street and started up the hill. Park Crescent was one of the better streets in the town, built between the wars then later extended in the seventies. Mature trees grew on the strip of grass between the pavement and the road and the houses were all detached, mostly bungalows with an occasional two-storey villa. The gardens were large and the hedges neatly trimmed.

'This isn't prostitute country, sir.'

'I know.' Smellie stopped. 'But if you lived in one of these houses you'd have very little idea of what was happening in the street after dark. Trees, hedges, curtains. In the dark I could knock you on the head and push you into the back of a Land Rover and who'd see anything?'

Cross looked around. 'I see what you mean, sir. We're almost invisible.'

They walked on until they reached George Beale's house, crossed to the other side and walked back down to the High Street.

'No evidence of tyre tracks on the grass,' Smellie said. 'No evidence of anything at all. But Laura Beale must have been attacked on this stretch of road.'

He used his mobile to call Sarah Noonan.

'I want a house-to-house both sides of Park Crescent all the way from the High Street to the junction with Ismay Place. We need to know if anyone saw or heard anything between eleven and twelve last night. We're especially looking for any sighting of a Land Rover van.'

There were three red flags inserted on the 1/50,000 Ordnance Survey sheet on the board in the incident room at Divisional HQ, one in the county town, one at the ferry terminal, one on the moors road five miles out of Garrmouth. They stared at the result in silence.

'Doesn't tell us a damn thing,' Fowler said. 'You could make all sorts of suppositions from this.'

'Two killings in Garrmouth is suggestive, sir,' Larch said.

'Agreed,' Fowler said. 'It suggests our man is in Garrmouth twice as often as he's in Brickhill. But what do we make of that?'

No one answered. Fowler looked around the silent faces. 'Have we anything from the lab yet on the tyre track?'

'Nothing yet, sir,' Pearce said.

'I want an answer now!'

'I'll call again, sir.'

Sarah Noonan infiltrated the group. 'Professor Shane is here.'

'My office,' Smellie said.

Professor Shane looked as if she had spent a goodly sum of money on her hair since Smellie had last seen her. She sat down and gave him a twinkling smile and he suddenly realized there might be a problem.

'Give us the rundown, Professor,' Fowler said.

'Not quite the same as last time,' Leonora Shane said. 'There's evidence of a pretty violent blow to the back of the head before strangulation occurred. The skin is broken and there's bruising but just a trace of blood in the hair. There's no sign of a struggle, no sign of the victim scratching her neck trying to get her fingers under the ligature.'

They stared at her. 'Any sign of sexual activity before death?' Smellie asked. 'Or afterwards?'

'No indication. Obviously a failed attempt to remove the panties.'

'And it was done with a length of blue polypropylene rope and a pound coin was found in the mouth,' Fowler said. 'The rope was exactly the same length as on previous occasions and was knotted at the ends in exactly the same way. What's different is that Laura Beale was not a prostitute but looked like the previous victims: tallish, slim, dark hair, black stockings. Or, in this case, tights, which look the same. Robbie, get that information to the forensic psychologist. Smellie, the husband is suspect, of course, and any man she was playing around with or refusing to play around with. Work on that. We need a report on the tyre print and we need sightings of vehicles on the moors road last night.'

Stewart Pearce entered Smellie's office and read from a piece of paper. 'The tyre print is from an Avon Ranger Mark II. Very common on off-road vehicles. This one appears to be pretty new.'

'Now we're getting somewhere,' Fowler said. 'Work on that, Inspector. I want a report immediately on all Land Rover vans with that tyre.'

Pearce displayed some printout paper. 'I've done that, sir, at least for all the Land Rovers checked out so far. Seventy-six of them have that kind of tyre.'

The meeting broke up; Leonora Shane hung back.

'I know you're busy at the moment, Bill, but maybe when you've found your strangler you could give me a call.'

'I could do that.'

Shit, he thought, watching her leave.

Smellie drove up Park Crescent, noting several police vans and cars and the officers carrying out the house-to-house enquiry. It would be surprising if anything useful turned up; the great British public knew remarkably little about what happened beyond its drawn curtains.

There were two cars parked in George Beale's driveway. A younger version of the bereaved husband answered the door. Smellie identified himself and DC Winston and they were ushered inside.

'I'm Graham Beale,' the young man whispered. He was pale and Smellie could feel the tremor as they shook hands. 'Dad's in the sitting-room. He's had quite a shock. My sister Carol is here as well.'

They dealt with the business of introductions and condolences; Beale's daughter was now Mrs Sanderson. Smellie apologized for intruding.

'I hate having to bother you right now, sir, but this is a murder investigation and we have a massive amount of work to do and we need to clarify one or two points.'

George Beale nodded silently, not taking his eyes off the baby on his daughter's knee. Smellie estimated its age at about six months and its gender as female, but admitted to himself that he could be wrong.

'Does it have to be right now, Mr Smellie?' the young woman asked. She was tall and slender with short dark hair. 'We're all a bit shattered.'

'It won't take long, Mrs Sanderson, and it's essential,' Smellie said. 'I'm sorry.'

'I should have collected her from the Marine,' George Beale muttered. 'I should have insisted. But she said she'd be late and not to wait up. It was midnight, one of the times they had their evening. But I wouldn't have minded sitting outside in the car till she was ready.'

'Were you at home all evening, Mr Beale?'

'Yes. Except to drive Laura down to the Marine at nine o'clock.'

'And you came straight back?'

'Yes. It only took ten minutes, so I left the computer on. We were thinking of going to Scotland on holiday next year, so I was searching through the Ordnance Survey atlas, looking at places to visit.'

'And when did you go to bed, sir?'

'Towards eleven, as usual.'

'Any phone calls?'

'I called at about half past ten,' Carol Sanderson said. 'I'd forgotten Mum would be out, but Dad was still awake. Why are you asking all these questions?'

'Routine,' Smellie said. 'It has to be done. We eliminate as many people as possible so we can concentrate on the ones that are left.'

Graham Beale sat up in his chair. 'You mean – Dad's a suspect?'

Smellie nodded. 'Automatically. He's not really a suspect, of course, but when wives are killed it's usually by their husbands, so we routinely eliminate the husband if at all possible.'

He looked round their faces and offered an apologetic smile. 'Sorry, but it has to be done. In this case, everything points to another murder by the man the papers are calling the Blue Rope Strangler, but I have to go through the procedure. Please don't be offended, Mr Beale. All we want to do is catch the man who killed your wife and the other two women. When you phoned, Mrs Sanderson, who answered?'

'Dad did, of course.'

'Did you talk for long?'

'A couple of minutes. It was nothing important.'

'Where do you live?'

'Eglinton Terrace. Number seventy-one.'

'And you, sir?'

'Norwich,' Graham Beale said. 'If it's relevant, I spent yesterday evening being question master at a pub quiz to raise funds for my local cricket team. About sixty witnesses, if you insist on checking.'

'Don't take offence, sir. I have a job to do.'

'Sorry.'

'I don't have an alibi,' George Beale said. He sounded completely uninterested. 'I can't prove I was here after Carol phoned. I was, but I can't prove it. Except the door was unlocked when you arrived this morning. I'd left it unlocked for Laura. I don't suppose that proves anything.'

Smellie watched Winston make neat entries in his notebook.

'And you didn't notice that your wife hadn't come home. What I mean is, you didn't lie there half-asleep waiting to hear her come in?'

'No.'

'Dad's famous for sleeping,' Graham Beale said. 'Eight hours a night, dead to the world, snoring like thunder. Carol and I both left home as soon as we could to get some peace and quiet.'

Smellie nodded. 'OK, that's it. Thank you for your patience. I won't need to trouble you again.'

Beale still seemed barely interested. He sat forward in his armchair and held out his arms towards his daughter and lifted the baby on to his knee and tidied her smock.

'You've no granny now, darling, but Granddad will make up for that. There are lots of wonderful things we can do together.'

8

DS Grossmith had been co-ordinating the house-to-house enquiries in Park Crescent. Faced with a Chief Detective Inspector, two Detective Superintendents and two Detective Inspectors, he was decidedly nervous.

'We checked all the houses as required, sir. Not everyone who would have been there last night was there when we were there, sir, if you see what I mean.'

'Understood,' Smellie said. 'Did you learn anything interesting?'

'It's a very quiet street, sir. The houses are set well back from the road and most of them have hedges and there are trees along the side of the road; lots of shadows at night, and it's not easy to see what's happening outside, especially with the curtains shut and the telly on. We didn't find anyone who saw or heard anything suspicious.'

'How about people walking dogs last thing?' Naismith asked.

'A few of these, sir. We asked if they would have recognized Mrs Beale and quite a lot of them would have, sir, because the Beales have lived there for years. But none of them saw her last night. None of them saw anyone on foot at about the right time, except two old guys walking their dogs who met and stopped for a chat.'

'Vehicles?'

'Three, sir, but no Land Rover. One Honda clearly identified as belonging to a Mrs Leigh, on her way to see her husband, who's in hospital and had taken a turn for the worse. One Peugeot which turned out to be a son visiting his mother.'

'What about the vehicle not clearly identified?' Larch asked.

'A dark-coloured saloon seen at about midnight, sir, by an old gent looking for his cat. No make, no number. It just drove past, going downhill towards the town.'

'Too late,' Pearce said.

Grossmith indicated frustration. 'We don't even know precisely what times any of these vehicles were seen, sir. Everyone's bloody vague.'

'Who haven't you spoken to?' Fowler demanded.

'Twelve people, sir. They're at work or away somewhere.'

'Talk to them.'

'Yes, sir.' Grossmith left with every sign of relief.

'It's your patch, Smellie,' Fowler said. 'Any ideas?'

'Questions rather than ideas, sir. I walked from the High Street, where the victim was last seen, as far as the Beale house. It took just four minutes. The weather last night wasn't too bad. So why did Mrs Beale allow herself to be enticed into a vehicle? She wouldn't have got into a vehicle with a stranger. She'd had a couple of drinks but she wasn't acting stupidly. So – either she knew the vehicle and the man who was driving it, or she wasn't enticed. She was forced. We know she was struck on the back of the head: it may be that the blow was struck while she was walking up Park Crescent.'

'Agreed,' Fowler said impatiently, 'but that doesn't get us any further forward.'

Smellie nodded. 'Not yet. But it raises the possibility that Mrs Beale knew the vehicle or the driver, or at least thought she knew the vehicle. We could follow that up. And there may be indications on the grass strip between the pavement and the roadway. I think we should do a close search for footprints or drag marks, anything at all. There was an indication of grass and soil on one of her shoes which may not have come from where she was dumped.'

'I'll go with that, sir,' Larch said.

'Do it,' Fowler said. 'Smellie, you're in touch with the family, so you find out if Mrs Beale knew someone driving a Land Rover van; Naismith, you organize Scene of Crime and some experienced officers to search the grass strips. Pearce, haven't you come up with anything on this bloody Land Rover?'

'We're working on it now, sir, trying to correlate vehicles with tyres and excluding the ones with definite alibis. We still haven't had time to visit every owner, but we have enough to get started. We're going to need a lot of manpower.'

'Break it down into divisions and get the local guys to do it. Every officer on the ground. You know what we're looking for. Eliminate then concentrate.'

Smellie phoned the Beale household and Graham Beale answered.

'Sorry, sir, but I have a couple of questions.'

'That's all right.'

'It didn't occur to me to ask if your mother had a job.'

'She went back to work just a year ago, when I got married and left home. Carol had already left, and Mum didn't fancy being alone in the house all day, so she pulled some strings and got a part-time job with the Social Work Department. Something to do with providing people with wheelchairs and ramps and so on. Disability aids, that's it.'

'Good. Now, did she know anyone who drives a Land Rover van? Does anyone in the family know such a person?'

There was a longish silence. 'I can't think of anyone, Mr Smellie. Wait: I'll ask Dad and Carol. They're here.'

Smellie waited patiently. The sky outside his second-floor window was brilliantly blue, the sea sparkling, but the people in the street were wearing scarves and had their collars turned up.

'Hello? Sorry, Mr Smellie, but we can't think of anyone Mum might have known who drives a Land Rover van.'

'Thank you, sir. Hopefully, I'll be able to leave you in peace now.'

Smellie went down to the incident room and sat beside Sarah Noonan.

'Does the Social Work Department in the town run any Land Rover vans?'

She moved quickly through several screens on her computer and scrolled down.

'They have three. Two short wheelbase and one longwheel-base. Green. Office use, which means it's not the same driver all the time.'

'Print me the details, Sarah.'

'Getting somewhere?'

'Who knows? Driver!'

'Sir.'

'Follow this up. Inspector Noonan will give you the details. Was this Land Rover available to a driver after hours? Who was in charge of the vehicle on the relevant nights? If you're suspicious of anyone, bring him in.' He paused and muttered something rude. 'No. The first thing you do is ask if the council logo is painted on the side of the vehicle, and if it is you say thanks and find something else to do. But make sure about the logo.'

Fowler, Larch and Pearce had returned to HQ. Almost everyone in Smellie's squad and a large proportion of Superintendent Parsonage's uniformed officers were out tracking down Land Rovers. Smellie ate a late lunch in the canteen and returned to the incident room swearing that in future he would bring sandwiches; it was the only form of self-defence available to him.

'Anything from Park Crescent?'

Sarah Noonan shook her head. 'They've done one side of the road and drawn a blank. But Langholm called in a minute ago, quite excited. He and Winston are in Fording: know it?'

'Ten miles south on the coast.'

'That's it. They made enquiries then withdrew and want assistance. They're suspicious.'

'I'll go. Where exactly are they?'

Smellie drove down the single street, the sea and a gravel beach on his left, the houses on his right. Small boats were moored in the bay or drawn up on the hard. Fording was a straggling village, part old fishing harbour, part posh retirement homes, with a few small businesses at intervals. It was on a loop road which meant it was spared the heavy traffic on the main coast road. He stopped the Mazda and walked forward to Langholm's Mondeo and got into the back seat. Langholm and Winston turned to look at him, their faces clearly excited.

'What've you got?'

'This was our eighth Land Rover check, sir,' Langholm said. He pointed towards the roofs of some greenhouses showing behind a house on the right. 'That nursery is run by one Adam Senior, age fifty-four; lives on the premises. He drives a Land Rover van, long wheelbase, green. It has Avon Ranger tyres, almost new. There's blue polypropylene rope wrapped round the front bumper. And there was evidence of soil and plant material on the rope used by the strangler, which would tie in with a nursery. We've spoken to him, and he gave us a pretty aggressive response. He says he was in the pub last Saturday night and at home watching television when Mrs Beale was murdered. He knows what we're on about.'

'Well done. Let's go talk to him again. Drive in.'

There was a short access, badly surfaced, leading to a white-painted bungalow with a red pantile roof. Langholm swung the car to the right and stopped in the centre of a dusty area surrounded by wooden sheds and the gable ends of several big greenhouses. A green long wheelbase Land Rover van was parked beside one of the sheds with its back door hanging open. A tall man appeared at the door of one of the sheds and watched them get out of the car.

Smellie displayed his warrant card. 'Good afternoon, sir. I'm Detective Superintendent Smellie, Garrmouth Division CID. You've already met these officers. We're investigating the murders of three women and I'd like to ask you some questions.'

'Ask away, but you're wasting your time. It wasn't me, and I can prove it. You're on a bum trail.'

He was tall and lean and fit-looking for his age, deeply tanned by the sun. Probably a whiz with the ladies, Smellie thought, noting the dark wavy hair worn overlong and the regular features and dark eyes. One of those people who look good in any kind of clothing, even a padded tartan shirt over a sweat shirt and scabby corduroys. The voice carried a hint of education and authority.

'Is there somewhere we could talk, sir, or would you prefer to come along to the station?'

'You're trying to intimidate me.'

That's true, Smellie thought. 'Not at all, sir. Is there somewhere we can talk?'

'You'd better come in the house. I could do with a coffee.'

They followed him round the side of the bungalow and in by the kitchen door. Adam Senior waved a hand to the table. 'Sit down. I'm sure you'll accept a cup of coffee.'

'Thank you, sir.' No woman, Smellie thought, looking around. Either that or a criminally untidy woman. Adam Senior apparently used a chopping board as a plate and his last meal had been soup and bread and butter: the remains were still on the table, surrounded by the scattered sections of *The Times*.

'I told your chaps I had alibis for the times of these murders, Mr Smellie. Isn't that good enough?'

'No, sir. We have various bits of evidence and you seem to match the profile very closely. That may be coincidence, of course, but we have to check it out.' Smellie caught Senior's eye and offered a smile of great innocence. 'I'm sure you understand.'

'Don't smarm me, Mr Smellie. Ask your questions, I'll give you straight answers, you can check them out and that'll be that.'

He took four mugs from the draining board, glanced into them and put them on the table. 'I'm hoping this won't go on long enough to justify real coffee, so we're having instant.' He dropped a handful of teaspoons on top of *The Times* and added a packet of brown sugar cubes. The electric kettle was beginning to sing. He leant back on the sink unit and folded his arms.

'OK, let's get started.'

'It's the Land Rover interests me most, sir. A vehicle exactly like yours was caught on closed circuit television at the time of the murder of Sandra Sim last Saturday night, and a tyre track was found at the spot where the body of Laura Beale was found up on the moors this morning. The same make of tyre as you have on your Land Rover.'

That hit home, Smellie thought, watching Adam Senior's face. I'm on to something here.

'Laura Beale?'

'Yes, sir.'

'She's dead?'

'Strangled. With a length of blue polypropylene rope, just like the other two women.'

'My God! I didn't know.' The kettle boiled and blew steam

across the kitchen then switched itself off.

'You didn't know, sir? It's been on the radio and the television.'

Senior shook his head. He looked completely at a loss for words. 'I didn't know.'

'Murdered last night, sir, then her body dumped up on the moors. As I said, strangled with a length of blue polypropylene rope, the kind of rope you have wrapped round the front bumper of your Land Rover. The rope we found at the scene of the previous murders was just like that, and the laboratory found traces of soil and plant material on these bits of rope. So you can see why we're so interested in you, what with you running a nursery.'

Winston was taking the notes. Langholm rose and brought the kettle to the table and filled the mugs then spooned coffee into the water.

'I knew Laura Beale,' Senior whispered. 'Years ago. When was it? It has to be more than twenty years ago.' He shook his head. 'You read about murders in the papers, but it's a whole new experience when someone you know is killed.'

Smellie stared at him. This was totally unexpected. 'You knew her?'

'That's what I said!'

'So if you'd stopped and offered her a lift she'd have accepted. She wouldn't have been suspicious.'

Adam Senior shrugged. 'I suppose.'

'In what circumstances did you know her, sir?'

Adam Senior sat down at the table and dropped three sugar lumps into his mug and began to stir.

'I used to be married. We lived in Ismay Place, off Park Crescent, in Garrmouth. At that time Laura Beale lived round the corner in Park Crescent. Maybe she still does. Did. Did she?'

'Yes.'

Senior nodded. 'There was a sort of social thing going on. Dinners, barbecues, golf, sailing, parties. My wife was into that sort of thing much more than I was, but that's when I got to know George and Laura. And that's about it. They were people I knew when I was a lot younger. End of story.'

'What did you do in those days, sir?'

'I'd just come out of the Navy and was trying to settle down to civvy street. It wasn't easy to adjust. Everyone I worked with seemed to be bolshie, with no respect for authority. I had several management jobs, but I wasn't getting anywhere, and things weren't too good between me and the little lady so we split up and I put everything I had into the nursery. And here I am. Still struggling. God knows where the years have gone.'

'Are you a religious man, sir?'

'What?'

'Simple question. Are you a religious man?'

'As it happens, yes. I had a strong religious upbringing, but over the years I've become disenchanted with the conventional forms of religion and these days I tend to work on a very personal basis with my Maker. He knows my problems and understands and forgives my failures.'

'You were married?'

Senior nodded. 'For about three years, after a very brief courtship. Unfortunately, the vision did not stand up to the reality of married quarters and my long absences at sea. I left the Navy in the hope that we might be able to save our marriage, but it didn't work. Janice was sweet but rather dull. Never seemed to grow up properly. So I walked out, as much in the hope of giving her the chance to make a new life for herself as anything else. We're divorced. I've no idea where she is now and I don't want to know. Well, maybe I do. I've often wondered.'

'And you knew Laura Beale. Were you in Garrmouth last night?'

'No.'

'Where were you?'

'Here. I worked until about nine in the greenhouses then made something to eat and watched television then went to bed.'

'Alone?'

'Yes.'

'So you've no witness to this.'

Adam Senior shrugged carelessly. 'Ask next door, both directions. They can see me when I'm in the greenhouses.'

'Did you make or receive any phone calls?'

'No, I don't think so. All my calls are business.'

'Where were you last Saturday night?'

Senior drank coffee. 'I delivered a load of stuff in Garrmouth late in the afternoon then came back here and walked down to the pub for a meal and a drink, then I got into a darts game and had a few more pints then came home and went to bed.'

'Can you be specific about times?'

Again the shrug. 'I probably reached the pub about eight. An hour for a drink and then a meal. An hour playing darts. I suppose I left some time between ten and half past.'

'Witnesses?'

'Dozens. Ask in the pub.'

Smellie nodded. 'We'll do that.' There would have been plenty of time for Adam Senior to drive to Garrmouth and kill Sandra Sim at about half past eleven. 'Where were you on the Saturday night four weeks ago?'

'No idea. Hell, do you know where you were on a Saturday night four weeks ago? Or any day four weeks ago?'

'Try.'

'No idea. The pub seems a likely bet. Maybe someone will remember.'

'Did you by any chance drive to Brickhill that day?'

'Could have done. I make regular deliveries to various places in the town.'

'Do you have any vehicle apart from the Land Rover?'

'No.'

'Do you use prostitutes?'

'No!'

'Are you in a relationship with a woman?'

Adam Senior brought cigarettes and a lighter from the breast pocket of his shirt. 'None of your damn' business.'

'It's my business, sir. Are you in a relationship with a woman?'

A cigarette was extracted from the pack and the lighter snapped. 'I'm friendly with a lady, yes.'

'Her name and address, please.'

'Why?'

'She may be able to confirm some of the things you've told me.'

'I don't want you embarrassing her.'

'If you refuse to give me her name and address, sir, I'll have to send my men all round the village asking if anyone knows who she is. Which would be more embarrassing for her than a discreet visit.'

Senior glared at him. 'That's bloody blackmail!'

'This is a murder enquiry, sir. We don't have time to waste.'

'Her name's Peggy Napier. Hollands House. It's just up the road a bit.'

'Thank you. Have you recently pulled your vehicle off the road on to the verge up on the moors?'

'I'm rarely up there. It's months since I went that way. And I don't recall ever stopping.'

'So there's no legitimate reason for a tyre mark similar to yours being found beside a dead body up on the moors. Thank you.' Smellie hesitated. 'These officers will drive you to Garrmouth Division police station, where you will be asked to make a formal statement. It's likely that a Chief Detective

Inspector Fowler will want to ask you further questions. I think you should anticipate being away from home overnight.'

'Now look here, man. . . .'

'Don't worry about your home and premises, sir; I expect there will be a large number of policemen here for some time to come.'

9

Smellie watched the Mondeo drive out of the nursery and reached for his mobile.

'Fowler.'

'Smellie, sir. I've just sent a man back to Garrmouth to make a statement. He fits the bill very nicely. I need a search warrant and Scene of Crime.'

'Do you, indeed. Smellie, there are six men being interviewed right now who fit the bill very nicely, and we're expecting more. Land Rovers are being searched, tyre casts taken, blue rope being sent to the lab. How good is your evidence?'

'Good enough to make this call, sir.'

Silence. There were voices in the background and Smellie guessed that Chief Detective Inspector Fowler was making dismissive faces to indicate the hard-pressed senior man doing his best to cope with an idiot subordinate.

'I'll put someone on to it, but God knows when it will happen. You'll just have to hang on there. Here's Larch; give him the details.'

Smellie returned to the house and walked from room to room, keeping his hands in his pockets, noting everything but touching nothing. Tidiness was clearly not one of Adam Senior's virtues, although there was a suggestion that he cleaned up at intervals. The bureau in the sitting-room was open, revealing an old typewriter surrounded by a pile of unopened letters, catalogues, a stack of invoices, a packet of long brown envelopes and a cheap A4 lined pad. It did not match the paper used by the murderer when he wrote to Robbie Larch. There was an assortment of pens and pencils in a mug with the handle broken off and an overflowing bookcase revealed Adam Senior's interest in matters naval and horticultural. There were also three Bibles, all well used, and a great many murder mysteries.

There was nothing feminine in the bedroom, and nothing contraceptive; the bathroom was a cold and unwelcoming place with a damp towel hanging over the edge of the bath. On a row of hooks at the back door were a Barbour jacket and a fawn duffel coat, both very old and distressed. On a shelf above them were a tweed hat, a tweed cap and a moleskin pork pie hat.

Smellie returned to the yard and worked his way through the wooden sheds, finding nothing of interest. Finally, he looked into the back of the Land Rover.

Some sacks, a stack of plastic seed trays, empty cigarette packets, crumpled chocolate wrappers; dried soil all over the aluminium floor; a tangle of blue polypropylene rope. He made no attempt to touch it. Dried soil and a mess of scrap paper on the floor of the cab, petrol station receipts and signed delivery notes in a shoe box on the passenger seat. The tax disc was a week out of date.

His phone rang. 'Bill, it's Robbie. Is what you have really good?'

'I'd be shot down in flames if I didn't take action.'

'OK. I'll bump you up the queue. It may only be a couple of technicians for the moment, but they'll bring a warrant with them. You'll have to use your own people for the search.'

'OK, Robbie. Thanks.'

It would take half an hour at least for anyone to arrive. Smellie called the office and found Naismith in charge.

'We may have found our man, Jimmy. Winston and Langholm are bringing him in to make a statement. . . .'

'He's here. I was going to call and ask if you wanted me to talk to him.'

'I just want him parked there for the moment. There are technicians and a search warrant coming from HQ. Senior's nursery in Fording. My car's across the road. Get some bodies out here, as many as you can lay hands on. Where's Sarah?'

'I sent her home. She was knackered.'

'Well, leave someone in charge; I want you here as well.'

He went out to the street and looked around and started walking south, reading the house names on the gates as he passed. Hollands House was the fifth property along, a handsome villa set in a garden which was probably a riot of colour during the summer. There was a late model BMW parked outside the double garage.

The woman who opened the door was in her forties, shapely and attractive, dark hair expensively styled. Regularly maintained, Smellie thought; one careful owner.

He showed his warrant card and identified himself and noted the wedding and engagement rings on her left hand. 'Mrs Napier?'

'Yes.'

'May I have a word with you?'

'Come in. What's it about?'

'It's about Adam Senior.'

She took his coat and ushered him into a comfortable sitting-room. They sat opposite each other in enveloping armchairs. Everything in this room is expensive, Smellie thought. And tasteful. Including Mrs Napier.

'This is just a chat, Mrs Napier. A police officer gathering background information. Is there a Mr Napier?'

'Not now. He was on that 747 which crashed off the coast of Spain two years ago.'

'I'm sorry.'

She made a gesture with a long hand. 'Time heals, eventually, to some extent. Why are you interested in Adam Senior?'

'I'm working on what the papers are calling the case of the Blue Rope Strangler. Mr Senior is one of several people who are helping us with our enquiries.'

He watched her reaction but learned nothing from the raised eyebrows. Peggy Napier seemed to be a lady in complete control of herself.

'You know Mr Senior, don't you?'

'It's a small village and he lives just a few doors down. I buy plants from him.'

'I mean, you know him on a personal level.'

'Not really.'

'He gave me that impression. I asked him if he was in a relationship and he said he was and named you.'

'Then he had no right to do so, Mr Smellie. I'm aware of his interest in me, but I have no interest in him.'

The paintings on the wall were intriguing. One oil in particular was of a very high quality. If I can avoid offending this lady, Smellie thought, I may be able to ask her about it. Trouble is, she's pulling up the drawbridge.

'Men can't judge men the way women can, Mrs Napier,' he said. 'He struck me as a man who would be attractive to women. Tall, lean, handsome, dark wavy hair, all to the Mills and Boon specification. Was I wrong?'

'Yes. He's not attractive. Don't ask me to define the problem, but he's not attractive to women. There's something creepy about him.'

'And you and he never had any kind of relationship.'

'Never. He has tried without success several times, in what

you could say was a routine sort of way, but I've done nothing to encourage him.'

'Thank you. Now, what else can you tell me about him? He's lived here for many years – what do people think of him?'

She watched the coal fire flicker and gave the question some thought.

'I don't know of anyone in the village who has got really close to Adam. He just isn't a man anyone could get close to. Not anti-social, not antagonistic, but difficult to like. Detached. A loner. He did all the things you're supposed to do in a small village, like going down the pub and playing darts and talking to people and turning up at the cricket matches, but he just never seemed to fit in. There was something odd about him. Shouldn't you be making notes, Mr Smellie?'

Smellie smiled. 'I'll do that when I leave, Mrs Napier. I didn't want to inhibit you. Do you know of any other woman he was seeing?'

'No. I may not have heard, but I doubt it.'

'Can you think of any specific incident or occasion which might sum up his character?'

'No. Which is revealing in itself, I suppose. He just didn't make any kind of mark on our lives.'

'Thank you.' He placed one of his cards on the arm of the chair. 'If you think of anything relevant, please call me. That oil there is intriguing. May I have a closer look?'

'Of course. It's an early Trevor Lambertson.'

'Now I see it.' Smellie stood up and studied the canvas. 'Something about it rang a bell. His style changed a lot over the years. Ludicrous way to die.'

'It was very silly. It did wonders for the prices, but I'd rather he'd gone on painting. Are you a collector, Mr Smellie?'

'In a very small way. I seem to be specializing in pastels these days.'

'I have a rather pleasant Elizabeth McIver in the dining-room. Would you like to see it?'

'Love to.'

It was half an hour before she opened the front door for him; by then he had been all over the house and seen all her paintings and advised her to increase her insurance and get advice from the Crime Prevention Unit about security. She was sitting on a considerable fortune. And by now they were talking much more naturally to each other.

'Thank you for your advice, Mr Smellie.'

'Thank you for the chance to see some beautiful paintings, Mrs Napier.' He stepped out on to the porch. Now?

'Wait.'

'Yes?'

She hesitated. 'I'd like to help you as much as I can, but I don't want to be embarrassed at a later date.'

'We're very good at not embarrassing people, Mrs Napier.'

She avoided his eyes, concentrating on the slim hand holding the door open, then reached a decision.

'I did actually let Adam Senior get a little closer than I may have suggested. It was about a year after Robert was killed and I was very lonely and depressed and it was Christmas and I suddenly became aware that I have hardly any family left. We never had children. I met Adam by chance in the street and we had lunch in the pub and I drank a little too much and he brought me home and I thought, yes, why not. But then I saw Robert's shooting stick in the hall stand and changed my mind and tried to laugh it off and pretend that coffee really meant coffee. He became quite annoyed. He left, but I was frightened.'

'Can you remember what he said?'

'A few cutting remarks about women leading men on. About morals and attitudes and why do women make themselves beautiful if not to attract men. I received a hand-delivered note the following day offering a fulsome apology and saying he had misunderstood and hoped this unhappy little incident would not spoil our relationship. After that, we pretended nothing had happened. He would occasionally suggest dinner or something and I would wag a finger and say something about keeping it platonic.'

'Do you still have the note?'

'No.'

'Thank you, Mrs Napier.'

It was now a little after eight in the evening. Silhouettes moved back and forth against the glare of the powerful lamps. Yet another car drew up in the street outside and Chief Detective Inspector Fowler stumbled down the access into the light.

'Good evening, sir,' Smellie said.

'What've you got, Smellie?'

'The Land Rover has been trailered off to the garage at HQ, sir, for examination. The inside of the van has already been gone over very carefully and various samples taken. No direct evidence of Laura Beale having been in it, but it will be possible to establish if anything on her clothing matches the dust and fibres in the van. There are several bits of blue rope which will be examined. The search of the house is complete, but everyone's waiting for daylight so they can work in the greenhouses and the nursery.'

'And?'

'Nothing much, sir. Several garments which may tally with what was on the video. No paper matching the letter, but seven brown envelopes which look like the one used when the murderer wrote to Robbie Larch.'

Fowler sniffed. 'That's not very good, Smellie. From what you said I'd expected more. Is your man still at the station?'

'Yes, sir.'

'I'll talk to him.'

'Anything further from the lab on Mrs Beale, sir?'

'The soil and vegetable matter on her clothes tally with what was found on the bits of rope from the previous murders.'

'Then. . . .'

'It looks hopeful, Smellie, but let's not jump the gun. We're still talking to a couple of guys who also fit the bill. We should do a house-to-house. . . .'

'It's happening now, sir. Inspector Naismith and I dealt with the local pub ourselves: Adam Senior thinks he may have been in there on the Saturday night four weeks ago. Blank stares, just. There are people who think he may have been there that night, but don't remember his being there at closing time. There's nothing to prove he couldn't have killed Karen Potter.'

Smellie and Naismith worked their way through an Indian take away in front of the computer screen in Smellie's office. Naismith sucked his fingers clean and tapped a key.

'Everything's possible, Bill. Senior could have been at all the locations at the correct times. The stuff on the ropes matches the stuff in his van. There are signs he's a religious nut, like the psychiatrist said. He knew Laura Beale from way back, so she'd have trusted him enough to get into his van.'

'Why did he kill her?' Smellie asked.

'She was slim and had dark hair and black stockings, like all the others, including your Mrs Napier, who may have had a lucky escape. Or maybe Laura Beale pissed him off some time when they were all doing their parties and barbecues and so on.'

'It's very vague, Jimmy.'

Naismith grinned. 'I do the vague bits and you sort them out.'

Smellie laughed and looked at his watch. It was well after midnight.

'I shouldn't imagine Fowler would be all that pleased if I

called down and asked him how he's getting on with Adam Senior.'

'This is your manor, Bill. You have the right.'

Smellie shook his head. 'Not politic, Jimmy. Nor is going off home for a night's sleep. But you could do that.'

'I'll hang around. A beer would be nice.'

Smellie opened the bottom drawer of his desk. 'I can't manage a beer, but I just happen to have found a bottle of Bell's and a bottle of soda. Would that do?'

'I'll force myself.'

The phone rang at six minutes to three.

'You still there, Smellie?'

'Yes, sir.' I answered the bloody phone, didn't I?

'I'll come up.'

Fowler entered the office followed by Robbie Larch and sniffed the air. 'Curry and whisky. It's like a bloody whore's kitchen.'

'There's some whisky left, sir.'

'So splash it around, Smellie. We've had a long day.'

There was another bottle in reserve.

'Glass glasses,' Larch said. 'Class. Cheers.'

'So what's the situation, sir?' Smellie asked.

Fowler swallowed half his whisky and yawned. 'We have grounds for keeping Adam Senior downstairs for the time being, but not for charging him. I'm convinced he's our man, but we need more. I got your message about this woman he claims to have had a relationship with. . . .'

'Mrs Napier,' Smellie said. 'She says there's no relationship, although he tried hard enough. She thinks he's weird. By the way, she's slim and shapely and dark-haired and happened to be wearing dark stockings or tights.'

'I put that to him. He just laughed and suggested she was

trying to protect her reputation. What do you think?'

Smellie nodded. 'It's a possibility. She's a lady with a strong grip on her public image.'

Fowler emptied his glass and pushed it across the desk towards the bottle of Bell's. Smellie refilled it.

'I've had to let him get some sleep,' Fowler said. 'His solicitor insisted. We'll carry on in the morning. Robbie, get on to the lab and tell them I want more ammunition.'

Smellie and Naismith walked across the empty car-park. The moon was bright in a cloudless sky.

'That's Jupiter,' Naismith said, pointing. 'And that's Saturn. If you had binoculars you'd be able to see a couple of Jupiter's moons.'

Smellie remembered a freezing night in Naismith's back garden, squinting through a telescope, eyes watering, nose running. It had been fascinating but uncomfortable.

'You still do that stuff?'

'These days, I work off a CD-ROM on the computer. Is Adam Senior our man?'

'We don't have enough to charge him yet, but I'll be surprised if he's not.'

'Fowler's excited.'

'Fowler wants an arrest. Badly. He's under a lot of pressure and he doesn't like it.'

'Everything fits.'

Smellie shook his head. 'Some things fit, Jimmy, but not everything. Right vehicle, perhaps, but that evidence is suspect. No Land Rover van was seen at the site of the murder of Karen Potter. The video evidence of a Land Rover van at the site of the murder of Sandra Sim is not conclusive. No Land Rover van was seen in the vicinity of the murder of Laura Beale. One tyre track has been found, matching the type of tyres on Adam Senior's van, but it was not clear enough to pinpoint any one tyre, and there are thousands of four-wheel-drive vehicles carrying these tyres and the print could have been left by a different vehicle entirely. Adam Senior seems to be a bit a religious nut, but so are a lot of other people. The rope in his van matches the rope used in the strangulation of the three women, but it was not cut with the same blade. I think I've spotted one or two other little problems.'

Naismith's lighter flared and lit up his swarthy face. 'People have been sent down for less,' he said.

'I'd rather be convinced.'

Naismith unlocked his car door. 'I'd been looking forward to this thing being tied up by tomorrow so I could get some sleep and some regular meals. You're saying I won't?'

'It's out of our hands, Jimmy. Let's wait and see.'

10

Adam Senior had been moved to Police HQ in Brickhill and was still helping with the enquiry. The morning news bulletins on television were already announcing the capture of the Blue Rope Strangler. A tired-looking Chief Detective Inspector Fowler was shown sitting at a table with Robbie Larch beside him insisting that at this moment in time no one had been formally charged with the three murders but he then went on to admit that the massive investigation was being scaled down and concentrated in certain areas. By mid-morning the media had latched on to the activity at the nursery in Fording and the road along the shore was packed with vehicles, and anyone prepared to answer the insistent knocking at their door was being interviewed about the mysterious man who drove a Land Rover van and whom no one seemed to like. The publican at The Greensman's Inn did a rapid search of the hundreds of photographs thumb-tacked to the walls in the public bar and made excellent money from the Press by selling pictures of Adam Senior in group shots of the darts team and the cricket team and various casual gatherings.

By midday, judging from the live reports from Fording and Brickhill, the Blue Rope Strangler was in custody and would shortly be formally charged. White-overalled forensics experts were shown entering and leaving the house and the wooden sheds and greenhouses and there was speculation that more bodies might be found buried somewhere in the nursery. Officers were shown carrying out a house-to-house enquiry covering the whole village.

Smellie, Naismith and Noonan watched the midday news then Smellie switched off.

'Enough,' he said. 'We have work to do.'

They drank coffee and tried to bring some kind of order to the routine business which had been postponed when the squad had to drop everything and concentrate on the murders of Sandra Sim and Laura Beale.

'The buggers knew we were tied up,' Naismith said. 'Nine daylight break-ins. Six vehicles stolen. At the last count, seventeen vehicle break-ins, and they're not all notified. A gang of teenagers rampaging along the High Street. A smash-and-grab in Preston Close. Eight muggings. I spoke to the Super and he reckons it will take his people a week to get things sorted out.'

'Concentrate on our own stuff,' Smellie said. 'How many officers in court today?'

'Three,' Sarah said. 'Everyone else is on duty. I've extended the no-leave, no-off-duty order for another day or two, until we get to grips.'

'Good. OK, let's not waste time talking about it: let's do it. Everyone will have to work alone – we can't afford to send the troops out in pairs.'

'I should get the incident room dismantled,' Sarah said.

'Leave it for the moment,' Smellie said. 'That's not urgent.'

'What are you going to do, Bill?' Naismith asked.

'Fowler was on about half an hour ago. He wants background on Laura Beale and the fact that Senior knew her, even if it was nearly a quarter of a century ago. Plus any background I can find in Garrmouth about him. I'll tackle that myself And I'll have to make a courtesy call on George Beale, for a start, to let him know what's happening. He shouldn't have to get it from the news on television And he'll want to know when he can arrange his wife's funeral and I'll have to explain we need to hold on to the body for a while yet. I hate this bit.'

'On your own, sir?'

George Beale nodded. 'For the moment. Carol has her own family to consider and Graham has a job to do. I insisted they go home. Can I get you some coffee, Mr Smellie?'

'Yes, let's have a cuppa.' Smellie followed Beale into the kitchen. The marmalade cat lay stretched out on the floor and did not move when they stepped over it.

The kitchen was like a photograph from a catalogue. It was the size of Smellie's sitting-room, with enough farmhouse-style pine cupboards to hold more than any family could possibly need. Beale pointed to a pine table with six chairs.

'Sit down, please, Mr Smellie. Instant all right?'

'Fine.'

George Beale's idea of casual wear was perhaps typical of the man. Razor-sharp creases on the dark-blue trousers, a white shirt and dark blue tie under a V-necked jersey, polished black brogues. His bald head reflected the light.

'I called to bring you up-to-date with what's been happening, sir.'

Beale indicated the portable television on a work surface. 'I see from the news bulletins that a man is helping police with their enquiries. That usually means an arrest.'

'We're hopeful, sir. The media have already found out who he is, but can't say anything just yet. I can tell you his name, if you promise to keep it a secret until there's an official announcement. It's someone you may remember – Adam Senior.'

Beale froze in the act of taking a mug out of a cupboard. 'Good God!'

'I understand you knew him when he lived in Ismay Place about twenty years ago.'

Beale nodded. He looked blankly at the mug then placed it on the work surface beside the kettle. His hand moved hesitantly then he shook his head and brought down a second mug and reached for a glass jar full of coffee.

'It was longer ago than that, I think. He and his wife were guests quite often.' He frowned. 'I can't remember her name. A pretty, fluffy sort of woman, not terribly bright but quite pleasant company. In those days, there were a lot of young married couples in the neighbourhood, young families, dinners, parties, barbecues. You grow out of that sort of thing quite quickly. Though I don't remember the Seniors having any children.'

'What was your opinion of him, sir?'

The kettle boiled and Beale made the coffee and laid the mugs on the table then brought a matching bowl of sugar and a jug of milk and two teaspoons and sat down.

'I seem to remember he was usually invited because his wife had been invited. He wasn't exactly great company. He'd been in the Forces, if I remember correctly, an officer of some kind, and he was having difficulty adjusting to civilian life. I think he had several jobs in quite a short space of time. A bit morose, usually. He always seemed to be complaining about something.'

He sipped his coffee and looked at Smellie. 'And you think he murdered Laura?'

Smellie gestured vaguely. 'At the moment the evidence justifies his being questioned, but we're a long way short of going to court. A tyre track up on the moors, beside where your wife was found. The fact that she seems to have been prepared to accept a lift when she was only a few minutes walk from home, which suggests that she had to know the driver. The soil and vegetable matter in his van and on your wife's clothes are broadly similar to what was found on the various bits of rope used to . . . . used by the murderer. It's not exactly an open and shut case. If Adam Senior had been driving down Park Crescent and stopped and got out and said something like, "Hello, it's Laura, isn't it?" how would she have responded?'

Beale examined his fingernails. 'Politely. Assuming she recognized him.'

'I doubt if he's changed much over the years,' Smellie said.

'She never liked him much,' Beale said. 'She liked Janice – I've remembered her name – but I remember her saying she didn't think much of Adam. If he stopped and offered her a lift . . . . I'm not sure. What was the weather like? I've forgotten.'

'Cold but not freezing. Dry.'

Beale shrugged. 'She might just have accepted a lift out of politeness; she might even have invited him in, I suppose. After twenty-odd years, she could have forgotten how she felt about him. Or he could have changed.'

'Did you ever meet him after he separated from his wife and moved away?'

Beale frowned and shook his head. 'I was barely aware he'd gone. I seem to remember someone telling me he'd started a business of some kind down the coast. He just sort of vanished after he and Janice broke up. I'd forgotten all about him till now. Why would he want to kill Laura?'

'We're hoping he'll tell us, sir.'

'You're not sure? But I thought. . . .'

'Enquiries are proceeding, sir. Did your wife colour her hair?'

Beale stared at him, caught out by this sudden change in the questions.

'Yes.'

'What colour was it originally?'

'Same as it is . . . . same as it was. . . . Black. The grey was beginning to show and she didn't like that.'

'So she didn't actually change the colour, she just maintained it?'

'Yes.'

'Thank you. Is there anyone still living in the neighbourhood who lived here when Adam Senior did? Someone who showed up at the parties and dinners and so on?'

'The Arbuthnots: third on the right in Ismay Place. The Seniors lived right next door to them. And Anna Anders, of course, in Park Crescent. I forget the number. Across and up a bit.'

'Was Mrs Arbuthnot a close friend of your wife?'

'Close enough. But Anna Anders was Laura's closest friend. She's separated from Norrie but she still has the house. If Laura had any secrets, Anna will know them, and I'm sure she'll be eager to tell you all about them. Anna is all mouth, as well as being thoroughly weird.'

'Mrs Arbuthnot?'

'Yes?'

Smellie displayed his warrant card and introduced himself. 'I wonder if I might have a word with you. I'm investigating the murder of Laura Beale.'

'Oh!' Tears immediately filled Mrs Arbuthnot's eyes and she urged Smellie inside with a flapping hand. She was a plump and untidy woman with, it seemed, a fondness for pinks and oranges and reds. The swelling bosom under the pink angora cardigan could have comforted an orphanage.

'Come through. . . . What did you say it was?'

'Mr Smellie does the trick. Thank you.'

She joined him on an overstuffed couch in front of a huge television. The screen showed the nursery at Fording. A reporter was talking urgently to camera.

'I've been watching all morning,' Mrs Arbuthnot said. 'Shall I turn the sound down?'

'Switch it off,' Smellie said firmly. 'If you want.'

She switched off reluctantly and stared at the blank screen. The blonde curls had been artificially enhanced and the blue eye shadow seemed inappropriate for the time of day.

'I don't feel safe now, Mr Smellie. I used to feel safe. Ismay Place is a nice, quiet street, but suddenly Laura's been strangled round the corner and I get a fright every time the bell rings.'

'Can you keep a secret, Mrs Arbuthnot?'

'Oh, yes!' Her eyes shone with anticipation. She would be on the phone to someone before he reached his car.

'The man helping us with our enquiries is Adam Senior.'

She stared blankly at him for a long moment then understanding dawned and she clapped plump hands over her mouth. 'Oh! Adam Senior? That used to live next door?'

'Yes. I'd like to take some notes, if that's all right.'

'Oh!'

He was about to ask for her opinion of Adam Senior then changed tack; Mrs Arbuthnot's opinion of Adam Senior was now based on the assumption that he had strangled Laura Beale.

'When Adam and Janice lived next door to you, what were they like as neighbours? I mean, did you visit each other, chat over the fence, have coffee together and so on?'

'Oh, yes. The houses were all new, you see, and we all moved in at the same time. We were all young married couples and we were all painting and papering and doing the gardens and having babies and everything. Janice was so nice, and the men used to help each other then go down the pub together and come back to someone's house and phone the wives and we'd all go round and have a drink and supper and so on.'

'What was Adam like in those days?'

'He was tall and thin and rather handsome, really. A bit quiet.

He'd been an officer in the Navy and I remember Willy – that's my husband – I remember Willy saying one night that Adam still acted like he was in the officers' mess, a bit of the class thing, but he was all right, really. There was the odd rumour that he was playing around, but I think that was just because he was tall and dark and handsome and you'd sort of expect it of someone like that.'

'How did he and Laura get on?' Smellie asked lightly, watching Mrs Arbuthnot's pale-blue eyes and noting the first hint of caution.

'I don't know.'

'It's important, Mrs Arbuthnot. Did you ever think there might be something between them?'

The awkward silence lengthened.

'Was there any specific incident that made you wonder if there was anything between them?'

The plump shoulders moved up and the double chins tripled. 'We had a barbecue one night and asked everyone round. Some of the men had been at a golf tournament and they'd already had a drink and it was quite lively. Willy was showing some of the men the sailing dinghy he was building and they'd sort of set up a bar in the garage and I went in with more sausages and on the way back I saw Adam and Laura climbing over the fence into Adam's garden. I stopped and saw the light from them opening his back door. They were away for quite a while and when I saw them again they were sort of making a point of not being together. But I'm not sure. . . .'

'And after that? You were suspicious, so you'd be aware of things other people might not have noticed.'

Mrs Arbuthnot nodded, her eyes avoiding Smellie's.

'Janice didn't notice, I don't think, and George didn't, but I could see what was going on. Touching and whispering in corners, looking at each other in that special way, sneaking off, going to each other's houses when they shouldn't. Listen, you promise you'll never tell George about this.'

'Did it last long?'

'No. A few months, only. Then things got bad between Janice and Adam and he got himself a flat in the town and not long after that we heard they'd separated. I suppose maybe Laura visited him there, but from what I heard Adam was really shattered about the marriage breaking up and was really depressed and was avoiding everyone.'

She seemed barely aware that Smellie was filling page after page of his notebook.

'Did Adam and Janice have any other close friends in the street?'

'The Findlays. Charlie was in the Navy like Adam. They were pretty close.'

'What's their address?'

'Oh, they went back to Scotland. But we still exchange Christmas cards. Hold on.'

The woman who answered the door at 75 Park Crescent was not exactly what Smellie had expected to find in the staid middle-class suburbs of a small seaside town.

'Hello, handsome.'

He grinned at her. 'Hello yourself and see how you like it.'

'Tom Sawyer, I think. Maybe Huckleberry Finn?'

'One or the other. I'm Detective Superintendent Smellie of Garrmouth Division CID, investigating the murder of, among others, Laura Beale.'

'And I was Laura's closest friend, which is why you're here. Come in, Chief Detective Superintendent Smellie of Garrmouth Division CID. Let's talk.'

11

Smellie walked past Anna Anders into the house and stopped. Most of the hallway was lined with mirrors. In the myriad reflections he watched her close the door and come and stand beside him. Her sculpted black hair barely reached his left shoulder and the hem of her canary yellow dress barely covered her knickers, leaving sturdy thighs all too visible in candy-striped tights. Applying the dramatic black and white make-up must have taken her half the morning. Anna Anders seemed locked in a time warp.

'Like it, Mr Smellie? But you're too young, I suppose, to remember the sixties.'

'I was about five, I think, when the sixties ended.'

'Lucky man. The sixties changed everything and you reaped the benefits. I hope you're grateful. Come on through.'

He followed her into what had to be the most untidy room he had ever seen. There was hardly a bare inch of horizontal or vertical surface still available. If Anna Anders had read all the books and magazines and newspapers which filled the room then she had to know everything there was to know. The screen of a PC glowed on a desk in one corner and a large gas fire popped in the hearth and there were cats asleep wherever cats could sleep.

She made room for him at one end of a couch by moving a protesting Burmese and a stack of books then sat cross-legged on the rug in front of the fire, revealing more underwear than he really wanted to see.

'So, Detective Superintendent Smellie, are you anywhere near finding Laura's murderer? Which I assume would also mean finding the murderer of those other poor women.'

'I know the television news broadcasts suggest we have, Mrs Anders, but—'

'I don't have television and I'm not addressed as Missis. I prefer Anders to Niblo, but not Missis, although we're not actually divorced. Just call me Anna, dear. What's your first name?'

'Bill.'

'Bill Smellie. Dead common. No one with a name like Bill Smellie is going to get big-headed about being a senior officer at a relatively young age. There must be a lot of other officers don't make Detective Superintendent so young. Or ever.'

'One or two.'

'And you don't look like a man who'd go kissing anyone's backside, so the conclusion is that you're intelligent and good at your job. Nice. Right: ask away.'

'I'll make notes, if you don't mind. What do you do, Anna?'

'That's not what you came to ask.'

'But now I want to know.'

She laughed and he realized she must once have been sexy but never beautiful.

'I don't have to do anything, darling. I used to write terribly clever articles for various highbrow magazines, and sometimes I still do, but Norrie left me for other women and instantly regretted it and he has money coming out his ears and feels guilty and pays off his guilt quite handsomely. He also sneaks home at regular intervals and pokes me in a friendly sort of way. My fourth book is due out in August. Yet another analysis of the sixties; I think I'll have to write about something different next time. You were going to ask about Laura.'

Smellie stared at her. Behind the bizarre appearance and lifestyle was an intelligent and level-headed woman.

'Did you know Adam Senior?'

'Yes. He was Laura's lover for a while. And mine, incredibly briefly.'

'Why incredibly briefly?'

Anna Anders smiled. 'Straight to the heart of the matter. I enjoy talking to intelligent men.' She rocked back on her haunches, gripping her ankles; the candy-striped tights were stretched to their limit. 'Why briefly? Because he was too intense. One night and he wanted it to be forever.'

'But you didn't.'

Anna Anders shrugged. 'He was nothing startling. Just another bloke. Anyway, I wasn't looking for a lover.'

'You were still with your husband at this time?'

'Yes, though by then I'd discovered Norrie had women like other men have a drink. This isn't relevant to anything.'

'Tell me about Laura Beale and Adam Senior.'

Anna Anders stopped rocking. 'With Laura, what happened was much more important. She married George with considerable ceremony but little passion. Not exactly an arranged marriage, you know, but not far short of it. The parents met and negotiated politely, according to Laura, then George was called in and informed of the corporate decision. We're not talking prenuptial agreements, but just about. I always got the impression that if George's shirt had been a different shade of white he might have had to do a resit. He'd clawed his way up through day release and evening classes, you see, instead of actually going to university. But he was a very determined bloke, and he made it in the end. Want a drink?'

'Yes.'

'There's whisky.'

Smellie waited. 'Whisky, then.'

'I think there's some wine in the fridge.'

'Whisky.'

Anna Anders heaved herself to her feet and left the room and returned with two mismatched glasses.

'I added a little water.'

'Fine,' Smellie said. '*Slainte*.' The water was not detectable, but the whisky was good.

Anna Anders chose not to resume her seat on the hearth rug. She cleared a cat and some more books off the couch and curled up next to Smellie.

'Do policemen make love?'

'Whenever they can.'

'With whomever they can?'

'No.'

'You have a lady?'

'Yes, thank you.'

'Bugger! Go on.'

Smellie grinned. It was impossible not to like Anna Anders.

'Tell me everything you can about Laura Beale and Adam Senior. Did they carry on their relationship after he left Ismay Terrace?'

'For a while. He got a flat in the town and she used to visit him there then they had some kind of fight and she stopped seeing him.'

'When did she see him last?'

Anna Anderson frowned and stared into space and ran her fingers rather obviously up and down her thigh. 'We're talking twenty-something years ago, Bill. The memory isn't that precise. I'd say it all stopped a few weeks after he left Ismay Place.'

'How did that affect her?' Smellie asked.

'I can't give you an eyewitness account, dear, because I was in the States with Norrie at the time, but she told me about it when I got back. I think she was relieved, really. The excitement had worn off and without that they weren't exactly a loving couple, and she was afraid George would discover what was going on and kick her out. Adam wasn't earning much and Laura liked her big new house. She didn't fancy pigging it in Adam's grotty little flat.'

'So George never knew?'

'No. I think Laura had had her little fling and decided it was time to settle down and be the dutiful wife of an up-and-coming young executive. She was a virgin until she met George, you see, and she had this nagging doubt that she'd missed out on something. I suspect Adam proved she hadn't.'

There were framed photographs packed tightly together among the paintings and drawings on the walls above the PC. Smellie pointed.

'I think I can see you and Laura together in one of those photographs.'

'Yes. Come and see my memory wall. I'm a lady who thinks in images.'

They stepped carefully over the piles of books and magazines and the sleeping cats.

'That's Laura and me in the back garden here.'

'When?'

'Just look at my waistline, love. About twenty years ago, probably.'

'So you weren't always a Mary Quant lookalike.'

'Darling! How old do you think I am?' She looked at Smellie with exaggerated offence. 'Don't answer that. I was too young to experience the sixties fully. I didn't really get into the sixties till the eighties. Does that make sense?'

'So long as it makes sense to you,' Smellie said, studying the photograph. Laura Beale was slim and attractive and wore her black hair curling over her shoulders. 'Did she always wear black stockings or tights?'

'She preferred them, yes. She had beautiful legs and she thought black or one of the darker browns showed them off. I rather think George liked them too. I think they turned him on, if you can imagine George Beale being turned on; appalling image. That's George and Norrie and me and Willy the day we launched Willy's home-made dinghy, which floated, much to everyone's surprise. He has a sailing cruiser nowadays and pretends he's Captain Blood the pirate.'

Norrie Anders, it seemed, was mostly hair and muscles. George Beale looked like a young man eager to reach middle age. The brown hair was already receding and there was even a suggestion of a crease down the front of his jeans.

'What does your husband do?'

'Drinks and eats and chases women.'

'For a living, I mean.'

'Oh. He's a photographer. He used to do weddings and families but moved into fashion and went to London and that's when I lost him. I miss him, sometimes, for short periods. Usually when there's a blocked drain.'

Smellie laughed. Join the police and meet weird people, he thought.

'Any family?'

Anna Anders shook her head. 'We kept putting it off till later, then there wasn't any later. I tell myself children would have interfered with my life. Sometimes I almost believe it.'

A black cat appeared suddenly on the desk beside the PC. It looked at Smellie then rose on its hind legs and put its paws on the front of his shirt and stared at him.

'Think yourself blessed, Bill. Jet is not friendly. You must have a way with animals.'

Smellie stroked the shining black fur. 'My dad was a village constable on the other side of the moors and people used to bring in stray animals. My job was to look after them. Cats, dogs, ferrets, ducks, goats, sheep, even ponies. When you're five years old you tend to treat animals as equals. I keep meaning to read a book on animal psychology, just to put words to whatever it was I did by instinct.'

He lifted the cat and settled it in his arms and it began to purr, its eyes half-closed.

'Well, that's definitely a first,' Anna Anders said. 'That's the first time Jet has allowed himself to be lifted. Let me take your glass. Let's have another.'

'I shouldn't.'

'Don't you ever do what you shouldn't?'

'I like being coaxed.'

'Is that what you tell your lady?'

'Yes.'

'I bet you have fun.'

When she came back he was sitting on the couch with the cat throbbing on his lap. She sat beside him and the cat hissed.

'Did Adam Senior strangle Laura, Bill?'

'That's what I was going to ask you.'

'I don't know.'

'Perhaps you do, without realizing it.'

She stared at him and sipped from the glass. 'After more than twenty years?'

'Laura Beale was one of three women,' Smellie said, 'all very alike in appearance, strangled in what was almost a ritualistic way. In other words, we're dealing with a man who is not right in the head. Someone obsessive, someone driven, someone with a compulsion. Adam Senior lives alone in Fording, runs a small business, reads three Bibles, has no woman friends. The only woman we know he's interested in is also slim and has longish black hair and on the day I talked to her she was wearing black stockings or tights, which may not be a coincidence. I know it's twenty-odd years since you knew him, but can you spot any connection, any influence, any peculiarity, anything odd that might help me?'

'Let me think.'

Smellie stroked the cat and drank his whisky, happy to give Anna Anders time to reflect. He respected her intelligence and wanted a considered answer. It was a full minute before she spoke.

'I remember one night Janice – she was Adam's wife – got a little bit drunk and got me alone on the bench in the back garden and said she wanted to ask my advice. Her question was, how often did Norrie and I make love in a month. I said I'd no idea, because I'm virtually innumerate, but it was once or twice a day and a bit oftener at the weekends and she could do her own arithmetic, allowing for periods, and I knew instinctively this wasn't the right time to mention what we did then. She was gob smacked, to put it crudely. This was news. I asked how often she and Adam did it but she never quantified the matter; however, I got the impression we did it oftener in a week than they'd done it since they got married, which was a couple of years or so earlier.'

'This is interesting,' Smellie said, 'but you're not answering my question.'

'I am, Bill, as best I can. Janice was a pretty little thing, blonde and blue-eyed, clear skin, good tits, good legs, very nice butt. Sexy. A lot of the men fancied her. But she didn't turn Adam on. Laura did. Make of that what you will.'

'I see,' Smellie said. 'I'll have to take advice. We have a forensic psychologist working for us.'

The cat wriggled over on to its back and stretched its front and rear legs in opposite directions, exposing its belly. Smellie scratched it with slow strokes. The purring became thunderous. Anna Anders shook her head in disbelief.

'I do not believe this. That cat was mistreated as a kitten, abused, starved, dumped on the street. I brought him home hoping I could at least give him some decent food and a relaxed environment, but I've never been able to get nearer to him than about three feet, and then he was hissing and the claws were out. How do you do that?'

'No idea.'

'You must know.'

Smellie shook his head. 'I don't think about it. They seem to understand me. They seem to know I care about them.'

'You can take him home, if you want.'

'I live in a third-floor flat and sometimes I don't get home for days at a time. I'd love to have some animals, but it's just not on.'

'Come and visit any time you want, Bill.'

'Maybe I'll do that, Anna.'

'Is your woman beautiful?'

Smellie smiled. 'She's tall and slim and has incredible legs and a great sense of humour and tolerates a policeman with irregular hours. And she's intelligent and a great cook. She's lovely.'

'You haven't actually said if she's beautiful.'

Smellie teased one of the cat's hind paws until the claws appeared. 'I don't know. I expect she is.'

Anna Anders shrugged expressively. 'I can't compete with that. Have I helped?'

'You've, given me useful information. You've helped bring Adam Senior and his wife and Laura Beale to life. Who else knew them in those days?'

'Margot Arbuthnot.'

'I've spoken to her.'

Anna Anders emptied her glass and balanced it on a stack of books. 'I suppose everyone knew something, but Margot and I were Laura's closest friends.'

'Did Laura play around with anyone else?'

'No. She'd have told me, I'm sure. We told each other everything.'

'Did Adam Senior play around with anyone apart from Laura? And yourself, of course.'

'I hardly count, dear. A quick poke after a boozy party. No, I don't think Adam had any other lovers. He wasn't exactly God's gift to women, you know.'

'Could George Beale have killed his wife?'

She stared at him. 'I can't think why. Why should he? A middle-aged couple with two grown-up children and a grandchild, big house, pots of money. He could just have waited for her to die of boredom. Why do you ask?'

'Routine. The husband is always the prime suspect when a wife is murdered.'

'Dead end, darling. George is slightly less than dynamic. I can't imagine him getting het up enough about anything to do something as momentous as killing his wife. Anyway, what about those other women?'

'Maybe it was a copycat killing and we have two murderers. No, I forgot, that wouldn't work. Certain secrets about the method.'

'Are you serious?'

'No, not really. But I do have to consider all the permutations. I've met Graham Beale; what's he like?'

'You're thinking of him as a suspect?'

'We automatically look at everyone close to the victim.'

'Graham is the kind of son I wouldn't have wanted, Bill. An adult while he was at school and rapidly approaching middle age in his twenties. No blots on his neatly ruled copybook. No drink, no drugs, no wild parties, no putting it about, at least so far as Laura knew. He'd decided to be an accountant before he went into secondary school. Passed all his exams, got qualified, got a good job recently. George was awfully proud of him.

Graham doesn't realize it, but he might as well die now. He's done everything he's ever going to do. I believe his sole remaining ambition is to become president or something of his cricket team. If that happens he may very well die on the spot of emotional surfeit.'

Smellie grinned. 'You don't like him.'

Anna Anders dismissed Graham Beale with an expressive gesture. 'Nothing to do with me. If you want to know if Graham killed his mother, check his income tax form. He'll have put the rope down as an allowable expense.'

Smellie laughed. The cat raised its head and looked at him without interrupting the purring.

'Do you know anything about where Janice Senior is now?'

'Janice lives in Liverpool these days with a social worker and has three children and runs a pre-school nursery. I doubt if she has the time to kill anyone. You're not learning much, are you?'

'Yes, I am,' Smellie said. 'Later I'll be able to pick out the bits that are relevant.'

'I thought Adam Senior had been nicked.'

Smellie laid the cat carefully on the couch between them and smoothed its whiskers.

'Perhaps he has been, by now, but we'll go on collecting background information for a while yet.'

They stood on the front doorstep and looked out at Park Crescent.

'Anyone else I should speak to?' Smellie asked.

'I doubt if anyone still here could tell you anything you don't already know, dear. Quite a few of our incestuous little group have moved on.'

He gave her one of his cards. 'If you think of anything I should know, call me, please. Thanks for the drink.'

'Come and visit, Bill. I like you. Bring your long-legged lady. And if you ever want a cat, or several, I have some to spare.'

'Thank you. 'Bye, Anna.'

Smellie walked out to his car and drove away. He stopped round the first corner and switched off the engine and went back through his notes, carefully elaborating on what he had learned from Anna Anders.

'Our incestuous little group'. It was an interesting phrase.

12

Smellie returned to his office and called HQ and asked for Robbie Larch. Stewart Pearce took the call.

'What's the score, Stewart? Has Senior been charged?'

'Not yet, sir. We're getting a magistrate's warrant to hold him a while longer. He's insisting he had nothing to do with it. The traces on the ropes match but the various bits of rope in the Land Rover and around the nursery were cut with Senior's pocket knife and the ligatures were not. The tyre print is too indistinct to be conclusive. The traces on Mrs Beale's clothes do match the stuff on the floor of the Land Rover and Fowler and Robbie are pounding away at that and the fact that Senior knew Mrs Beale years ago.'

'They were lovers.'

'What? Beale and Senior?'

'Yes. Over a period of several months, a long time ago.'

'Wait, sir. I'll interrupt.'

There was a delay of several minutes then Fowler came on the line. 'Smellie? What've you got?'

Smellie gave him a concise but detailed account of what he had learned from Anna Anders and Margot Arbuthnot. Fowler listened in silence.

'Well done, Smellie. I'll want all this in full on paper immediately. I understand the inquests have been fixed?'

'Friday, sir.'

'You handle that. And see if you can get me any more background information on Adam Senior, anything I can use. He's being bloody stubborn.' The phone went dead.

That, Smellie thought, was the nearest I've ever known Norman Fowler come to being gracious. An important day on the calendar. He flicked through the screens on his PC and began to type. When he had checked the spelling and replaced some of the large words with simpler ones he printed and took the results through to one of the DCs and asked for the sheets to be faxed to CDI Fowler.

Naismith joined him at the coffee machine. 'Anything happening?'

'Adam Senior and Laura Beale were lovers in the dim and distant.'

'That's interesting. So she'd have got into his vehicle. And he drives a Land Rover van.'

'Yes.'

'How did their affair finish up? Badly?'

'I don't know how he felt about it,' Smellie said. 'The word I have is that she was glad it was all over. She'd had her fun and she didn't want to compromise her marriage. Her husband was a rising young executive, but her lover was a descending young failure, and everything indicates Laura Beale was a lady with an acute eye for the material advantages.'

'You think Adam Senior was after revenge?'

'Twenty-odd years is a long time to harbour a grudge.'

'But he's a weirdo, Bill. No woman, a Bible-basher. . . .'

'So maybe we should arrest every Roman Catholic priest in the county.'

'You know what I mean.' Naismith lit a cigarette and blew the smoke away from his friend. 'Maybe the killings of Karen Potter and Sandra Sim were deliberate, but the killing of Laura Beale was spur of the moment. Just her bad luck he was driving down Park Crescent when she was going home. He recognized her and decided to go for it. He'd already killed two prostitutes and he was in the mood, flushed with success, over the edge.'

'I don't like coincidences, Jimmy. If you're suggesting he was actually out looking for her, I'll go with the idea. If she wasn't his target, I'm left wondering where he was going and what he was planning at that time of night.'

'Good evening, M'sieu Smellie. Good evening, Mademoiselle Grey. Your table eez ready.'

'*Merci* Gaston.'

Jane watched the diminutive figure summon a waiter then bustle away. 'You were going to do it. Why didn't you do it?'

They were convinced Gaston's excessive French accent was fake and it was a standing joke between them that Smellie should engage him in conversation in French to see what would happen.

Smellie shrugged. 'If he really is French, I'll be embarrassed. I'm not as fluent as all that. And if he's not French, he'll be embarrassed and we won't be able to come back, which would be a pity, even at these prices.'

Jane giggled. 'You're soft.'

'Except when I'm with you.'

'I want steak. You can afford it now you're a chief constable or whatever it is.'

'I want steak too. I haven't had a decent meal for ages.'

They avoided shop talk until they were walking the short distance along the silent streets to Smellie's flat.

'Has this guy Senior been charged yet?' Jane asked.

'No. I've a suspicion he will be, but I wouldn't like to go to court on what we have so far. We need more.'

'So what are you going to do?'

'We think one of the murders – Laura Beale – may not be

random. She was his lover years ago. So we're going to check to see if he had any connection with the other two women at some time in the past.'

'Any unsolved murders on the books that might be connected?'

'It doesn't look like it. Robbie Larch has been plumbing the depths of the Police National Computer but nothing matches.'

They began the ascent of the stairs to Smellie's flat.

'I felt relieved when I heard he'd been nicked,' Jane said. 'You've no idea how nervous a lady gets when there's a strangler on the loose. Every dark corner, every unidentified noise.'

'You have your pink belt in tai-kwan-do or whatever it is. Maybe if these other ladies had done a little training they'd be alive today.'

'Are you sure none of them did?'

Smellie stopped and stared at her. 'That's not really relevant, but I should have asked what training Adam Senior had. He was in the Services: maybe he had special training in unarmed combat. Do they strangle people in the Navy?'

Jane pushed him up the stairs. 'Later. For the moment any unarmed combat is going to be on a more personal level.'

'Be gentle with me. Well, reasonably gentle. Hell, be as rough as you want.'

Anstruther opened the door of Smellie's office and looked in.

'Adam Senior's service record, sir.'

'Come in. Learn anything?'

'Yes, sir. Mr Senior specialized in shipboard electrical systems.'

Smellie stared at him. 'That's it?'

'Yes, sir. No special training in unarmed combat. Some training in first aid and fire control, but no one taught him how to strangle people.'

'How remiss of them. OK, thanks. By the way, you did a good job searching for patterns. It all seems to have been a waste of time, but that often happens in this job. Hopefully, you'll have learned something.'

'I did, sir. I'll tackle it differently next time.'

'And you made a new friend.'

Anstruther blushed. 'Yes, sir.'

'Good. Carry on. Tell Mr Naismith I want to see him.'

Naismith entered carrying two mugs of coffee and sat down. 'Morning.'

'Morning. What's happening?'

'We're tackling the backlog.' Naismith closed his eyes and used his fingers to keep track while he rattled off everything the members of the squad were doing. 'And Sarah's called in some bodies from upstairs to dismantle the incident room and Langholm and Cross and I are about to get started on trying to find a connection between Senior and Sandra Sim. Someone at HQ is already doing that with Karen Potter.'

'Good. The inquests on the murdered women are set for Friday morning; you take care of that.'

'Right. What'll you be doing?'

'Fowler wants more background on Adam Senior. I've already infiltrated the Park Crescent social scene, so I'll keep going. I may have to ask George Beale if he knew about the affair between his wife and Senior, but I'll postpone that for the time being; no sense in making the man any more miserable than is strictly necessary. There has to be someone else who knows something.'

There was nothing useful in the computer against Adam Senior: two parking tickets and a late road fund hardly made him a strangler. One warning two years before about a faulty head-lamp, another in June about balding tyres. All these incidents had happened in places and at times which did not relate to the murders.

Smellie phoned George Beale's number but there was no answer; he called Beale's office and was told that the ferry terminal manager would not be in for a few days because of a family bereavement. There was no answer from Graham Beale's home number. The daughter, Carol Sanderson, was at home.

'Detective Superintendent Smellie here, Mrs Sanderson. I've been trying to get hold of your father.'

'He's in London, Mr Smellie. He went up this morning to break the news to Gran. That's Mum's mother, lives in Wimbledon. She's a bit shaky these days, since Granddad passed on, and he didn't want to do it over the phone. We're just hoping she hasn't seen anything in the papers.'

'I see. Any idea when he'll be back?'

'Depends on the trains, I suppose, and how Gran takes it. Late afternoon, probably. Why?'

'I'm still trying to get background information on Adam Senior. The fact that he knew your mother a long time ago is something we can't ignore.'

'Well, what do you want to know?'

'It was all before you were born, Mrs Sanderson.'

'I know, but I lived in Park Crescent all my life until two years ago. I knew Mum's friends.'

'All right. I've talked to Anna Anders and Margot Arbuthnot. Can you think of anyone else your mother was close to, someone who lived in the area all those years ago?'

He heard what sounded like a sad little laugh coming down the line. 'Margot and Anna were certainly Mum's friends – and mine, I suppose but there were more. A delicate situation, sort of. People who were friends with Mum but not with each other.'

'Who were these people?'

'Hello Bill. I knew you'd be back. Made up your mind?'

'Hello, Olivia.'

He had attended the viewing of the Shand Gallery's latest exhibition two weeks earlier and had been strongly tempted by the two small oils showing the interiors of tenement staircases with curving stone steps and high, bright windows. They were still on the wall, no red dots on the cards. And the prices were still punitive. And they were in matching frames and ought to be bought as a pair.

And it was a waste of time haggling with Olivia Shand.

'Coffee, Bill?'

'Love that.'

She went through the back and he moved round the shop, studying the other paintings and pastels and ceramics and turned wooden bowls. This was the Shand Gallery's Christmas exhibition, deliberately aimed at people buying for friends and family, and there was some beautiful stuff. A large pastel by an artist he already had at home was very good but it was the two oils he wanted.

'Sit down, Bill. Still want the two Robert Hogans?'

'You know I do. Swap you: information for a sale.'

She rested her chin on her hands and her elbows on the desk. Today the briskly short blonde hair had a touch of amber in it.

'Must be the Blue Rope Strangler,' she said. 'Is it?'

'Yes.' He dropped brown sugar lumps into his coffee and left them to melt. 'This is secret, for the moment, but we have Adam Senior at HQ helping us with our enquiries.'

The green eyes widened in astonishment. 'The Adam Senior who used to live along from me in Ismay Place?'

'The very fella.'

'Good God!'

'We know Senior and Laura Beale had an affair way back, when he was living in Ismay Place. That's the only connection we've been able to make between Senior and the murders, apart from some doubtful forensic evidence. What can you tell me? Carol Beale, now Sanderson, tells me you and Laura were good friends in the past.'

Olivia Shand killed time stirring her coffee and lighting a long cigarette. He knew from past experience that she rarely spoke without thinking carefully about what she was going to say.

'Laura and I met when I bought my first house, in Ismay Place. I got friendly with Margot Arbuthnot and she invited me to one of her parties and Laura and I liked each other. In those days I was still very circumspect about my sexual orientation. You had to be, at that time, in a town like this, in a nice street like Ismay Place. I was found out after about a year and there was the inevitable polarization. Margot and Helen and Rosemary dropped me; Laura and Anna Anders and one or two others didn't have the same problem. I moved shortly afterwards, to the flat I'm in now, but Laura and I kept in touch. Anna as well. She's a one-off. Anna is not someone you could embarrass.'

Smellie stirred his coffee and sipped. 'Now tell me about Laura Beale and Adam Senior.'

Olivia Shand laughed. 'He was a man not getting enough at home. He propositioned me twice in one week. The fact that I lived alone seemed to make me a valid target, I think. I remember literally holding him at arm's length and saying something like, "Why don't you go home and make love to your beautiful young wife?" and him saying, "She does nothing for me. I've discovered I don't like blondes".'

'But you're blonde,' Smellie said.

'Out of a bottle, darling,' Olivia Shand said. 'These days, it would probably be grey if I let it grow in, but it used to be very dark.'

'I have to make notes,' Smellie said. 'Do you mind?'

'I prefer to be taken seriously.'

'I know Laura and Adam Senior had an affair,' Smellie said. 'Were you aware of that?'

'Yes. She told me.'

Smellie paused and replaced the cup in the saucer. 'That's a surprise. I thought she'd have been very secretive about it.'

'Well, I'd guessed and I hinted about it and she told me. I think she was eager to tell me. Heterosexual ladies have this innocent trust in homosexuals, Bill; they tell us everything, assuming we won't pass it on except to our friends, and no one talks to them.'

'Did George Beale know?'

'No. Definitely not. George was a nice chap, generous and amiable and helpful but very naïve, very innocent. Trusting. He was honest and thought everyone else was honest. Especially his wife. He loved her, you see, and was very proud of her. He simply couldn't imagine her having an affair with another man. It made Laura feel very guilty, I think, that she was two-timing such a nice bloke. He wasn't exactly God's gift to women, and he could bore for a living, but he was a decent man and worked hard to make a good home for them and he trusted Laura and she felt bad about betraying him. I think she was glad when the affair ended and she could go back to trying to make it up to him. So far as I know she was faithful to him all the years since then.'

Smellie flicked back through his notes and drank the coffee.

'Were you aware of any antagonism between George Beale and Adam Senior?'

Olivia Shand shook her head. 'You're asking if I noticed any indication that George knew Adam had been screwing his wife. I've told you: the answer is no. I can clearly recall George going round to help Adam move house when Adam and Janice broke up. That was when the affair was at its most passionate. I really felt for George at that time. He was the perfect cuckold.'

'Who else knew?'

'One or two. God knows how far the news travelled.'

'Any indication that George was sleeping around?'

'No. Definitely not. George is one of those people who make promises and keep them.'

'What was the problem between Adam Senior and his wife?'

Olivia Shand stroked the fine skin on her cheek. 'I got on very well with Janice. She was beautiful, but she wasn't too bright. It was glaringly obvious that she and Adam should never have got married, but she never understood that. He simply didn't like her. I really don't know why they got married in the first place, except that she was infatuated with him and he was at sea for long periods and kept coming home in a seriously frustrated condition.'

'Was Janice unfaithful?' Smellie asked.

'Never.'

'You're sure of that?'

'Certain,' Olivia Shand said. 'Absolutely certain. She simply wouldn't have known how. Maybe, in a different world, she and George Beale would have married and lived happily ever after.'

Smellie finished writing in his notebook. 'The marriage broke up and Adam Senior moved to a flat somewhere in Garrmouth. Do you know where?'

'Endersley Street. Don't ask me for the number, because I've forgotten, if I ever knew. Laura used to visit. I used to give her a lift, sometimes, because she didn't have a car in those days. But by that time all the excitement seemed to have died down and she seemed to be doing it out of habit as much as anything else. Then Adam moved and the whole thing died a death. Or perhaps vice versa.'

'How did she feel about that?'

Olivia Shand ran her fingertips round her lips and stared through the big window at the passing traffic.

'I think she was relieved. I think she was finished with Adam Senior. Though I'm not sure he was finished with her. He kept trying to get in touch with her. From something she said, I think she had to read him the Riot Act, convince him it was all over. He wanted her to come and live with him in his pathetic little flat, but she wanted to stay with George and the nice house and the garden and the car. I don't think Adam quite matched up to her idea of the up-and-coming young middle-class couple.'

Smellie finished his notes and his coffee. 'Can you think of any reason why Adam Senior should strangle Laura Beale twenty-something years after they were lovers?'

He expected a quick answer, but Olivia Shand hesitated. He waited.

'I got the impression from Laura that Adam was very intense,' Olivia said. 'He wanted her to come and live with him when he broke up with Janice, but she refused. She ended the relationship but he kept calling her, stopping her in the street, writing to her, trying to persuade her to come and visit him. She refused, she told me, although I think she actually went once or twice. Then she insisted it was all over.'

'Bad feeling between them?'

Another long pause. 'Yes.'

Smellie left the gallery half an hour later with the two paintings encased in bubble wrap. £460. They would fit nicely, one above the other, in the corner of the sitting-room between the large pastels. Maybe, in time to come, he would learn not to feel guilty about buying art.

What the hell? Other people spent similar money on cars, or clothes, or foreign holidays, or model trains, or women.

He stopped in the action of opening the boot of the five-year-old Mazda and looked down at his baggy cords and the scuffed waxed cotton coat and reflected that he had spent his last holiday in a cottage in Skye with Jane and she had insisted on paying half the rent and he had never had a model train.

He walked down the street to the florist and arranged for a large bunch of mixed blooms to be delivered to the office where Jane worked as a solicitor. That way she could enjoy the flowers and also the pleasure of the rest of the staff being impressed.

Good move, Smellie, he thought. Now you don't have to feel so guilty. And there will probably be a pleasant little gesture of gratitude. You can look forward to that.

13

Using the address provided by Margot Arbuthnot, it took only a few minutes to track down Janice Senior, now using the name Locksley. Smellie noted her home and work numbers off the screen. When she answered he could hear the strident uproar of small children in the background.

He introduced himself. 'I'm sorry to call you at work. Would it be better if I called you at home during the evening?'

'It would make conversation a lot easier. After seven, if you can manage that, please.' She had been in Liverpool long enough to pick up some of the distinctive accent.

Smellie replaced the phone and flicked through his notebook. Carol Sanderson had given him two names, one of which tallied with what he had learned from Margot Arbuthnot, and he suspected he would just hear the same tale yet again. But Fowler would ask if he had talked to everyone and he had to be able to say yes, he had, all sources had been questioned.

The computer coughed up Charles Findlay's number in Perthshire. A woman with a strong Scots accent answered and listened to Smellie's preamble.

'My husband's at work, Superintendent. Do you want to call him there?'

'What kind of work is it? Should I be interrupting?'

'He's a writer. He works in a shed at the bottom of the garden, but he'll take a call if it's important.'

If it's desperately important, she seemed to be saying. Life or death at the very least.

'It's very important, Mrs Findlay.'

'Wait.' He waited, listening to the silence then the clicks.

'Findlay.'

Smellie introduced himself yet again. 'You may have read in the papers about three murders committed by the Blue Rope Strangler. . . .'

'I don't read the papers.'

'Perhaps you've seen something about it on television . . . .'

'All I watch is the football.'

'Let me bring you up to date,' Smellie said, keeping the irritation out of his voice, 'then I'll ask you some questions.'

He outlined the story so far. Findlay listened in silence.

'So?'

'Do you remember Adam Senior, Mr Findlay?'

'Of course. Long time ago, but he and I spent three years on one ship and you can't help getting to know a man in a small officers' mess. Then we happened to find ourselves living in the same street and we renewed the. . . . Not the friendship. The acquaintance.'

'I note the qualification, Mr Findlay,' Smellie said. 'You didn't like him?'

'I didn't dislike him. We spent time together but we never got really close.'

'Tell me about Adam Senior.'

'Why?'

'He's helping us with our enquiries. We need background information.'

'You think he killed these three women?'

'That's what we're trying to find out,' Smellie said. He waited for a response but nothing happened. 'If you were writing about Adam Senior, Mr Findlay, what would you write?'

Over the line he heard the sound of a lighter and the puff of smoke being blown.

'Would you like me to write something? I prefer to work that way.'

'All I want is your opinion of Adam Senior as a man and a few notes on how things were between him and Laura Beale twenty-odd years ago. And anything else you think might be relevant.'

'I'll do a piece. Give me your fax number.'

Smellie and Naismith met in the public bar of the Eastern Drifter.

'Two pints and two lunches,' Smellie told the barman. There was only one lunch available in the Drifter. They took a table in a corner well away from the fruit machine and Naismith opened his notebook.

'We showed Adam Senior's photograph to all available working girls in the town. None of them recognized him. I called Stewart Pearce and he told me they hadn't found any evidence that Adam Senior had done business with anyone up there. Dead end.'

'How reliable is that?'

'That's the question I kept asking. The consensus is that a tall, lean, handsome bloke in a Land Rover van would have been noticed and remembered. No one remembered him.'

'So he didn't use prostitutes. I suppose that would tally with him hating them enough to kill a couple of them.'

'Laura Beale?'

'That seems to have been personal,' Smellie said. 'There's enough evidence to suggest a revenge killing.'

'You're happy with that?'

'No. But I'm pleased you referred to a consensus rather than a consensus of opinion.'

'You explained that to me.' Naismith frowned. 'Redundancy. Right?'

'Well done.'

'What've you been doing?'

'Talking to a couple of people who knew Laura Beale and Adam Senior when they were lovers. There's a Scots bloke going to send me something in writing. He's a writer and that's the only way he works, for heaven's sake. Sounded like talking was an effort.'

They watched the waitress slide two plates on to the table. Each carried one battered fish, with no room to spare. She hurried off and returned with two large bowls of chips and two ramekins of tartar sauce and a bowl of mushy peas.

'In London,' Smellie said, 'they manage to get a whole fish supper on one plate.'

'Clever buggers,' Naismith said. 'Makes you feel dead provincial.'

Charles Findlay seemed to work quickly. His fax was delivered to Smellie early in the afternoon, concise, spell-checked and grammatically correct. Smellie read through the three sheets of paper then punched out the numbers on the phone.

'Thank you for the information, Mr Findlay. Very clear and concise. I note you kept in contact with Adam Senior after he left his wife and took a flat in the town, until you left yourself about four months later. What was his mood like at that time?'

'Depressed. Partly because he felt guilty about leaving Janice, partly because Laura didn't go with him.'

'Had he expected her to do that?'

'Yes. It was mainly why he left Janice.'

'He told you that, or are you guessing?'

'He told me. He was half-cut at the time, otherwise he might not have. He wasn't a great talker. We enjoyed some pleasant silences.'

'Can you recall his being angry with Laura Beale?'

'Yes. That one time, anyway. He felt he'd been suckered, that she'd promised him something but not delivered and he'd committed himself and she was probably laughing at him behind his back.'

Smellie glanced through Findlay's fax. 'You say George Beale was unaware of what was going on. How many people did know?'

'Just me. And I didn't tell anyone, not even the wife. And I didn't learn about it until Adam moved to the flat.'

You're unaware of the feminine urge to share a secret, Smellie thought.

'One final question, Mr Findlay: was Adam Senior a religious man?'

'Yes. Used to take Bible class on board ship.'

'Thank you. I probably won't need to bother you again.'

Dr Peabody's assessment of the strangler had been scanned into the computer. Smellie read through it again and compared it with his notes and typed out a quick update for Fowler, suggesting that the forensic psychologist should be asked for an opinion. Then he went back and erased the suggestion, knowing that the Chief Detective Superintendent was likely to take it as an impertinence. A polite request to be kept informed of Dr Peabody's reaction to this new information was more politic.

He sat back in his chair and stretched and sighed and closed his eyes and yawned.

There was a lot against Adam Senior, but there were problems. He began a mental list.

'Wish I was a superintendent,' Naismith said.

'I was deep in thought,' Smellie said, opening his eyes and blinking.

'And here's me thinking it was snoring I was hearing.'

'I was thinking aloud. And it's "were", not "was". It's a subjunctive or something like that, I think.'

'It were snoring I were hearing?'

' "Wish I were a superintendent".'

'But you are a superintendent.'

Smellie raised his hands in surrender. 'We'll talk about this again some time in the future. Have you brought me some coffee?'

'Sorry.' Naismith used the phone. 'Coming.'

'Jimmy, tell me you've found some hard evidence against Adam Senior.'

'No. But don't we have enough by now? What have you learned from your contacts in the posh suburbs?'

Smellie pushed Charles Findlay's fax across the desk. 'This guy lives in Scotland, but he used to be close to Senior. I've spoken to him, and I've compared what he says with the letter from the strangler and the forensic psychologist's assessment. You could say it all hangs together.'

Naismith read Charles Findlay's piece carefully while the coffee was delivered.

'OK,' he said. 'It's pretty good. There are definite signs of paranoia in Adam Senior: money or love but nothing in return, the feeling that women are laughing at him behind his back. And there's the religion bit: it's in the letter, and Adam Senior had three well-used Bibles in his bookcase.'

'And he used to take a Bible class on board his ship,' Smellie said.

Naismith spread his hands expressively. 'There you go.'

'Sounds like you're trying to persuade me,' Smellie said.

Naismith hesitated. 'That's the way it sounds? I wasn't.'

'Yup. I'd rather hear about Land Rovers and tyre tracks and blue rope and soil on Laura Beale's clothes matching the soil in Adam Senior's van.'

'Well, there's that as well.'

'Not really.'

Naismith frowned at Smellie. 'The soil and vegetable fragments are pretty definite.'

'Agreed,' Smellie said. 'But there are countless other permutations to cover that circumstance. It will take more than that to get a conviction. The Land Rover's uncertain, the blue rope won't hang him, the world is full of religious nuts or even sincere believers, and paranoia is not a crime. We can't go to court on what we have. Any half-competent brief would shoot us down in flames.'

'They were lovers. . . .'

'A quarter of a century ago. We'd have a job proving a crime of passion after that length of time.'

Naismith sighed noisily. 'So?'

'Don't ask me,' Smellie said. 'I don't know. I have two more contacts to talk to. One of them happens to be Adam Senior's wife, but all the indications are that she knew less about what was going on than anyone. I'm not optimistic.'

He called Liverpool from home that evening.

'I'm sorry I couldn't speak to you earlier, Mr Smellie. I daren't take my eyes off the children for a moment. If they're not swallowing something likely to choke them then they're biting each other.'

'No problem, Mrs Senior,' Smellie said, deliberately using her married name and waiting for a response.

'It's a long time since I was called that. I'm divorced now and using the name Locksley, although we're not actually married.'

'Mrs Locksley, then. But you were married to Adam Senior.'

'Yes. What. . . ?'

'Are you aware of the three murders in Garrmouth? The Blue Rope Strangler?'

'Yes.'

'Adam Senior is helping us with our enquiries.' He listened to the startled reaction. 'Are you surprised? By what has happened, I mean. Are you surprised that your former husband may have killed three women?'

Her hesitation lasted just a moment too long. 'Yes, of course.'

'I know it was a long time ago, but did you ever, in the time you lived with him, see anything in his character that worried you? Was he ever violent towards you?'

'No, never.'

'Was he a loving husband?'

'No.'

Smellie waited. The tone of her voice had suddenly become matter-of-fact. No emotion.

'I'm to blame, Mr Smellie. I'm not very clever. I'm not an intellectual. I fell in love with Adam before we met. He came to a party at a friend's house, in his uniform, just back from sea, and I flipped. He was something out of my dreams. I suppose you could say I went for him, and I got him. I asked to be introduced to him and when we met I turned on the charm like it was a tap. And whatever sex appeal I had. I made all sorts of assumptions about him, like he was experienced and sophisticated and mature, but in fact he wasn't. He was a virgin and scared of women. We had one night together then he went back to sea and we wrote long letters to each other and by the time he came back I'd wangled things round to accepting his proposal of marriage without him actually asking. We got married and we had a rather sad little honeymoon then he went back to sea again.'

She stopped. Smellie guessed from her voice that the tears had started. He wondered what Mr Locksley was doing.

'Go on, please.'

'I talked him into leaving the Navy. We both knew things weren't right between us, and we agreed it was because he was away at sea all the time and we needed more time together. But it wasn't that. We bought the house in Ismay Place and he got a job with a firm doing security systems and we made lots of friends and everyone round about was having babies but we were. . . .'

Smellie listened to the silence. 'Things weren't too good between you?'

A wet sniff. 'He was tall and handsome and attractive. I was young and everyone said I was pretty. It should have been good between us. But he didn't . . . you know. He didn't find me attractive. I thought it was my fault.'

Let her talk, Smellie thought. Give her the chance to get it out. She's probably been waiting for this chance for years. But Janice Locksley had gone silent.

'Were you aware of his involvement with Laura Beale?'

'Later. I wondered, at the time, but it wasn't until he left home that Margot Arbuthnot told me. I didn't believe her, but Anna Anders said it was true.'

'What did Adam tell you?'

Another long silence and the sound of a sniff. 'He wrote to me. No address on the letter. Sorry, sorry, sorry, not my fault, all his fault, big mistake, I could have the house and the furniture, please forgive him, not good enough for me, all that shit. He said he'd met someone and knew she was the only woman for him and it would be a waste of time trying to make our marriage work when he was in love with someone else. And good luck in the future. That's the bit broke me up more than anything else. Good luck in the future.'

'How did you react?' Smellie asked.

'Like a very young wife who loved her husband and he'd just left her for another woman. I was twenty-one years old and I'd only ever slept with one man.'

Smellie heard the rumble of a man's voice in the background.

'I must go,' Janice Senior whispered. 'Stan's getting upset.'

'Wait,' Smellie said. 'Who did you talk to about all this?'

'My mum. No one else. Till now.'

'Has Adam been in touch with you since he left you?'

'Not a word.'

'How are things with you these days?'

Her voice changed immediately. 'I have three children and I've just discovered I'm going to be a granny and that doesn't make me feel in the least bit old.'

'Thank you, Janice. Good luck. 'Bye.'

Smellie closed the call then connected to the Liverpool police and asked for a run-down on Stanley Locksley.

Smellie introduced himself yet again. 'May I come in?'

'Yes, of course. I doubt if I can stop you, and I'm not sure I want to. Come through to the lounge.'

Dark shoulder-length hair; immaculate make-up; a narrow waist and mobile hips under the soft woollen dress; slim ankles and tan court shoes; the flash of bright red on the fingernails.

'Sit down, Mr Smellie. I'm just having a small refreshment. Gin and tonic. Can I get you one?'

'Thank you, Mr Liddescroft. Easy on the gin. I'm still working.'

14

'You're still working at this time of night? Unfair.'

'A policeman's lot, whatever that is.'

The drink was served in a crystal glass with ice and a slice of lemon. Gordon Liddescroft sank gracefully into an armchair and crossed his ankles.

'You've caught me out, of course, Mr Smellie. I was expecting a visitor, but not you. Not a stranger. All rather embarrassing. I'd take the wig off, but I look ridiculous in a dress and make-up and a short back and sides with a bald spot. I take it this has something to do with the ghastly murder of Laura Beale and those other two women?'

'Just that. Your name was given to me by Carol Beale, who is now Mrs Sanderson.'

'I was at the wedding. In a suit, I may say. I don't lack the courage of my convictions, but I didn't want to embarrass the dear girl.'

Smellie swallowed some of the gin and relaxed in his chair. The room was restful, beautifully decorated, uncluttered. A bonsai on a low table seemed to be the centre point.

'What's that?'

'Japanese maple. It's about fifteen years old. I grew it from seed.'

'It's beautiful. I have no interest in horticulture, Mr

Liddescroft, but even I can see it's lovely, although I think I may just be seeing it as a work of art.'

'Thank you. That's what it is. Are you trying to get me relaxed?'

'Yes.'

'You're managing very well. As it happens, Olivia Shand has mentioned you to me. She has a high regard for you, which is a point in your favour. Olivia can be quite penetrating in her assessments of people.'

Smellie grinned. 'Being a regular customer probably helps. You knew Adam Senior and Laura Beale back in the days when Senior lived in Ismay Place. . . .'

'Yes. And I knew they were up to no good long before Margot spotted it, whatever she thinks. I take it Adam Senior is the mysterious suspect helping the police with their enquiries?'

'How did you work that out, sir?'

'I didn't. A lady friend told me.'

'That name is still supposed to be secret.' Smellie sipped his drink. 'Tell me about it. This is important. I'm trying to find out if Adam Senior had cause to murder Laura Beale.'

Gordon Liddescroft stroked the hair at the side of his face. 'Oh, he had cause, all right. She treated him abominably. Not at the start, of course: at the start it was a meeting of like minds, or perhaps some other parts of the anatomy. Adam had at last found a woman who turned him on and Laura had discovered illicit passion. Janice did nothing for Adam, despite the fact that she was a very beautiful and sexy young woman; George was a decent and upright young man but he didn't exactly light a fire under Laura. She was so embarrassingly virginal, even after they married. In an ideal world Adam and Laura would have met before either of them got married and they would have made their little mistake and split up having learned something useful and gone on to greater things.'

'So why did Adam Senior have cause to murder Laura Beale?'

Gordon Liddescroft placed his glass on a small table and lit a cigarette and frowned.

'Perhaps I'm overdramatizing. Nevertheless, what I heard was that Laura took what she wanted from Adam, then dumped him. By that time he'd left poor little Janice and moved into a flat in the town in eager anticipation of Laura joining him there, but she didn't. I know she visited him, because Anna Anders told me, but she also told me Laura had never meant the sorry business to go so far. All she was trying to do was to make herself feel credible in her social group. In those days, being a virgin when you got married was seen as an admission of ordinariness. One was supposed to be modern and have a bit of a past, but Laura was the product of a desperately conventional small-town family and listened when her mother told her she'd never get a good husband if she wasn't a virgin when she got married.'

'You still haven't told me why Adam Senior should want to murder Laura Beale.'

'Yes, I have. Adam was in love with Laura, but all she wanted was enough illicit sex to satisfy herself that she hadn't missed out on something. She felt it was her due. She didn't like feeling naïve. With Adam, it was a great deal more intense. He went out on a limb for her, burned his boats, crossed his private Rubicon and any other cliché you care to apply. He left Janice in possession of the house and half their joint money, which meant the loss of a pretty major investment. And Laura reacted by giving him a cheery two fingers as she went back to George.'

'It was that simple?'

'So far as I know.'

The doorbell sounded. Gordon Liddescroft looked unhappily at Smellie. 'Excuse me. This has to be the guest I was expecting.'

Smellie listened to the indistinct voices and heard the sound of a door closing quietly somewhere in the flat. When the elegant figure returned he emptied his glass and rose.

'I'll be off. Here's my card. If you can think of anything else that might be relevant, please call me.'

'I'll do that, Mr Smellie.'

They went to the door and Liddescroft unhooked the latch. 'It's George I feel for, even after all these years, Mr Smellie. A decent man who loved his wife, but she wasn't good enough for him. The one saving grace is that he never knew. Laura came to her senses and they had two lovely children and now they have a grandchild and everything's all right. Maybe that's the way it should be.'

'You're convinced he never knew?'

'Definitely. Some people have a marvellous innocence which protects them from the old slings and arrows. It's quite easy to be jealous of them. The funny thing is, these people seem to win out in the end. The more cynical of us spin our tangled webs and eventually we're defeated and give up from sheer exhaustion and the innocents prevail. It's a lesson to all of us.'

'Thank you.' Smellie wondered what to do next. Offering his hand seemed somehow inappropriate. ' 'Bye for now.'

He went down the stairs and stood on the pavement, feeling the raw wind on his face and smelling the salt tang in his nostrils. There was a sparkle of frost on the roof of his car. What was this? Thursday? If he had time at the weekend he would see about buying a warm coat of some kind. One of Jimmy's anoraks, perhaps. Jane would advise him.

I'm getting nowhere, he thought, recognizing the signs. Farting about, getting useless answers because I don't know the right questions to ask. If Adam Senior had killed Laura Beale twenty-odd years ago it would have been understandable, but waiting twenty-odd years just doesn't make sense. Something must have happened recently, something which made a change, started a process, stirred an old anger, whatever. And the best source of information has to be Adam Senior.

He drove back to the station and went up to his office and called HQ and found Robbie Larch.

'Hello, Robbie. I don't suppose Adam Senior has confessed everything yet, has he?'

'No such luck, Bill. We're struggling. The only solid evidence we have is the soil and vegetable matter on Laura Beale's clothes, and if we went to court we'd have to admit there are hundreds of places she could have picked up traces like that. The tyre track is the right brand but there isn't enough detail for a positive match. Blue rope is blue rope, but Senior's rope was cut with his pocket knife and the strangler's ropes were cut with a very sharp blade and Senior doesn't have one of these, although he may have got rid of it. We hammered the fact that there are traces of soil and vegetable matter on the bits of rope found wrapped round the necks of those women and on Laura Beale's clothes, and he runs a nursery, but he kept saying you'd expect that, what with ropes often being dragged about on the ground. We haven't been able to break him on anything. I think we're going to have to release him. I don't even think we can hold him till Saturday.'

Even with a magistrate's warrant ninety-six hours was the maximum length of time Adam Senior or any other suspect could be questioned without being charged. Four-thirty p.m. on Saturday was the deadline.

'Did you ask him if he'd had any contact with Laura Beale recently?'

'About a hundred times, Bill. Same answer every time. No meeting, no sighting, nothing on paper, no phone call, no birthday cards, nothing. Why?'

'It's this business of the twenty-odd-year delay,' Smellie said. 'I can't accept the idea of Adam Senior just happening to see

Laura Beale in the street one night and killing her. It's too much of a coincidence.'

'We worked hard at that angle, Bill,' Larch said. 'As you say, too much of a coincidence. So we worked on the assumption that he knew where she lived and had been watching out for her, maybe stalking her.'

'But. . . .'

'I know. No Land Rover van seen in the area, no one seen hanging around, and Laura Beale's night out was literally a once-a-year event he couldn't have anticipated. A bloody monstrous coincidence.'

'What do you think, Robbie? What's your gut feeling?'

'He killed these women. Very cleverly. Probably after a lot of planning. I know his house and his paperwork are a shambles, but his greenhouses and plants and watering system and everything are in perfect order. Meticulous. He can organize anything that really matters to him. Like a few murders. Have you nothing new for us, Bill?'

'I've talked to some more people who knew Adam Senior and Laura Beale when they were lovers, but all I got was confirmation and reinforcement of what I'd already heard. Senior couldn't make it with his wife, he could with Laura Beale, he committed himself, left his wife, rented a flat, then Laura Beale backed out of the agreement, if there ever was one. She went back to her husband, leaving Senior spitting nails. He was angry, but no one I spoke to remembered him threatening revenge. And, of course, for twenty-odd years there was no attempt at revenge. That's the bit I can't get round. Doesn't make sense.'

'Unless he just flipped, Bill.'

'Did he strike you as a man who'd flipped?'

'No. He has a temper, he's impatient, he resents being questioned, but he's sane. I think.'

Smellie pressed the button to switch on his PC. 'Anything from Dr Peabody?'

'She's consulting Professor Hendrikson. Her carefully qualified preliminary assessment is that Adam Senior matches their original profile, if you make allowances. Load of crap.'

'I can't think of much more I can do at this end, Robbie.'

'Try, Bill. Don't give up. Talk to people in the street, if you have to. Unless we can come up with something new, we're buggered. And he could do it again.'

Smellie replaced the receiver and tapped in his password then went through to the big room. Cross and Langholm were on duty.

'Coffee on?'

'Yes, sir,' Cross said. 'Reasonably fresh. Any news?'

'Adam Senior will be back on the street by Saturday at the latest unless we can come up with something new.'

They stared at him expectantly. He shrugged.

'Don't look at me. So far as I can see we've covered everything that can possibly be covered, unless you guys have any ideas?'

'What's the situation at present, sir?' Langholm asked. Smellie summarized.

'Is there anyone else you can talk to who knew Adam Senior in those days, sir? That seems to be our only source of information.'

Smellie added sugar to the mug and sipped and made a face. It would have been better if he had just gone to Jane's place and. . . .

'I've talked to a lot of people who knew both Senior and Laura Beale, but you're right, there must be other people. Trouble is, I'm at that stage where I'm getting pretty much the same story from everyone, just slanted differently according to the individual. People see things from their own point of view and put their own interpretation on events. But I'll keep trying.'

He went back to his office and settled down to inputting the results of his interviews with Gordon Liddescroft and Janice Senior. Finished, he faxed copies to CDS Fowler then started on a selective review of the evidence so far. It was almost midnight when he sat back and stared at the screen and blinked and yawned and wiped his eyes. He reviewed the pages he had created then saved and switched off and picked up the phone.

'You still awake?'

'Either that or someone else is answering my phone. I'm watching a movie.'

'I'm badly in need of someone to make me some toasted cheese.'

'I could manage that, lover.'

'With maybe some beetroot and tomato?'

'Even that. And Dijon mustard and horseradish and some onion rings and garlic.'

'God, but you're sexy!'

Naismith watched Smellie pushing coloured pins into the Ordnance Survey 1/1250 sheet on the board.

'Either there have been an awful lot of murders overnight or you're selling double glazing.'

'These are the people I've talked to who knew Adam Senior when he lived in Ismay Place. Lots of gaps. There must be people who know something.'

Anna Anders looked surprisingly ordinary in distressed jeans and a sweatshirt with a rude logo.

'Hello, Bill. Welcome back. Come on in.'

He followed her into the awful sitting-room. The PC was on, the screen showing lines of text.

'Coffee, dear? It's a bit early for a drink, even for me.'

'Coffee would be fine, thanks, Anna.'

'Dig yourself someplace to sit.'

There was a family of kittens in a cardboard box on the rug in front of the gas fire. The mother was a moth-eaten black and white moggy with vengeful eyes. When Anna Anders returned Smellie had two of the kittens in his lap and the mother was sitting on the rug grooming her ragged fur.

'You've done it again, Bill. You're the first human being to lay a hand on those kittens. I tried.' She displayed a large plaster on the back of one hand.

Smellie accepted the mug of coffee and stroked the head of one of the kittens. The blind eyes flickered and it uttered a pathetic squeak.

'I talked to Gordon Liddescroft last night. He reckons he knew about Adam Senior and Laura Beale before Margot Arbuthnot did.'

'That's what he told me, too. We met in the town yesterday morning and I told him you might be calling.' She sat cross-legged on the rug.

'I'm still struggling for information, Anna. We're going to have to release Adam Senior shortly unless we can come up with something definite. Was there anyone else, back in the days when you all knew each other, who was close to him and might have talked to him after he left Janice? Someone he might have confided in?'

'You've talked to Charlie Findlay?'

'Yes.'

'He was the nearest thing to a friend Adam had. Talk to Janice?'

'Yes.'

'And Gordon, of course.' Anna Anders reached out a hand to the moggy and withdrew it quickly in response to an aggressive hiss. 'There were others, but I can't think of anyone who ever got close to Adam. In fact, apart from Charlie, only Laura ever got close to him. What did you learn from Charlie?'

Smellie shrugged. 'That Senior was badly cut up about Laura not keeping her side of the bargain. That he was angry and hurt.'

'After all this time. . . .'

Smellie nodded. 'That's what puzzles me. If Adam Senior hated Laura that badly, why did he wait more than twenty years before he killed her? And what about the other two women? Can you think of anything that might have happened recently to change things? Anything Laura might have mentioned to you? When did you see her last?'

'Just a week or so before she was killed. She phoned over and invited me for coffee and a chat. She had a day off. And she didn't say anything about Adam or anything unusual happening or any problems. It was just chat.'

'Had she met anyone recently, anyone she hadn't met for a long time?'

'Don't think so.'

The cat stalked across the rug and rose to put its paws on Smellie's knee and sniff at the kittens. He ran the back of a finger across one ragged ear and she purred.

'Another first,' Anna Anders said. 'You're magic, Bill. You should have animals.'

'Who else can I speak to who might have something useful?'

'George and Adam had a sort of strained friendship. I think there was some talk once of Adam getting a job on one of the ferries. I remember George arranging for him to go on a crossing in the engine room.'

Smellie laid the kittens in the box and stroked the moggy's back. 'I can see me having to ask George Beale about his wife's lover. I don't want to do that.'

'Please don't, Bill. Spare him that. It would break him.'

Smellie rose and went to look at the photographs on the wall behind the PC. He was by now able to recognize George and

Laura Beale, Adam and Janice Senior, Margot and Willy Arbuthnot, Anna and Norrie Anders, Gordon Liddescroft, Charles Findlay.

'Who are these people?'

Anna Anders joined him and slipped an arm through his; he felt one breast being pressed against him.

'That's Moira Findlay with Charlie. Malcolm and Sonia something or other: they weren't here long. The Beales *en masse*: have you met the children?'

'Yes.'

'The Nicols: they're still here, but they were just on the periphery. Alec and Linda Robson: they went to New Zealand. Sam and Gretchen Lowe: he died not long after that photograph was taken. Peritonitis. That's the Bainbridges: he went off to France to work and never came back and she went home to her folks and I lost touch. The chap with Gordon Liddescroft was called Alan, I think. That was a long time ago. Now, that guy's name escapes me. . . .'

She withdrew her arm suddenly and stared at him, sensing his reaction.

'What is it?'

'An idea,' Smellie whispered. 'Just an idea. May I borrow this one?'

'Of course.'

'Thank you, Anna. I must go.'

When he reached the car he checked his notebook, found the number he wanted and called Carol Sanderson. She was at home and he was welcome to visit.

The house was clearly a first-time buy, one of a long street of similar houses, many of them with raw earth where gardens would eventually be created. Carol Sanderson was standing at the window with the infant in her arms when he parked the car outside and walked up the slab path. She opened the door and invited him in.

'Sit down, Mr Smellie. Coffee?'

'I've just had a cup, thanks, with Anna Anders.'

She placed the baby on the rug and sat down. 'How is she? She comes to see Marie every couple of weeks.'

'She's fine,' Smellie said. 'A real character. She seems intent on providing a home for all the stray cats in the town.'

Carol Sanderson laughed. 'We're just waiting till Marie gets a bit older then we'll take a couple of them off her hands. Our cat at home, Duke, is one she talked Mum and Dad into taking.'

'When did Anna's husband last visit? Do you know?'

'Norrie? No idea. Why didn't you ask her?'

Smellie shrugged. 'Never occurred to me till later. It's not important. Do you know if your mother met Adam Senior recently?'

'No. I mean, no I don't know. She might not have mentioned it. Why should she? I never met him.'

Smellie leant forward and put his finger in the baby's tiny grasp. 'She's lovely.'

'Isn't she? Trying to crawl but not quite getting the hang of it. She can sit up without falling over too often. It won't take long.'

'How long have you been married?'

'Almost a year.' She watched Smellie's face. 'And Marie is seven months old. We were quite prepared to go on living together, but Dad was keen that we got married so we did.'

'How did your mother react?'

'She was with Dad, but just out of loyalty, I think. She knew about Keith and me and she didn't mind.'

'Is that your wedding photograph on the bookcase?'

'Yes. With a little careful tailoring I was able to get married in church.'

Smellie rose and bent to study the photograph. 'You look

great,' he said. 'How is it young women always manage to look like film stars on their wedding day?'

'Excitement, I think.'

The infant was beginning to make threatening noises.

'I'll leave you to the mysteries of coping with a baby,' Smellie said. 'I think she's sprung a leak.'

'Is that all?'

'Yes, that's it. No: one more thing. Can you think of anything unusual happening at home during the past few months, something that made you wonder, some kind of change in the normal routine?'

'I got married; Graham left home to start work in Norwich; I had the baby; Mum and Dad became proud grandparents: that's a pretty abrupt change in their lifestyle.'

'Did they adapt easily to the change?'

Carol Sanderson looked puzzled. 'Why shouldn't they? It's a slow process. They had plenty of time to adapt.'

'Your mother didn't suddenly feel her age? I've known some women of her age take badly to becoming grandmothers. It makes them feel old. Especially attractive women like your mother.'

Carol Sanderson drew breath to speak then hesitated, frowning. 'You may be right, Mr Smellie. Maybe I was too mixed up in what was happening to me to understand. When you're pregnant and getting married and looking for a house and a mortgage you suffer a bit from tunnel vision. All you can see are your own problems.'

'Thinking back, then, do you think you noticed a change in your mother's behaviour?'

'Where's all this leading, Mr Smellie?'

Smellie sat on the arm of the couch. 'A peculiarity of a murder investigation is that the only person you can't question is the victim. So you have to ask the people who knew the victim best what she was like, how she felt, what she was doing and so on, trying to build up a picture, hoping to get to know her, hoping for some kind of insight, some flash of revelation, something to help you understand. Did you notice a change in your mother's behaviour, or your father's, or in their relationship?'

Carol Sanderson picked up the baby and cuddled her, stroking the smooth, plump cheek with a finger.

'Graham and I both noticed something. We talked about it and decided it was just Mum and Dad adjusting to being alone together in the house, without us to think about and cook for and look after and have around. We thought it would be a pleasant change for them.'

'What sort of change was it?'

She shrugged and looked uncertain. 'Just a general sort of edginess. It was mostly Mum, I think. She was always pretty direct and man-to-man with Dad, but recently she seemed more, I don't know, sort of eager to please, somehow. Graham and I decided it was because Dad was the only person she had to care for at home and he was getting her full attention for a change.'

'Can you pinpoint when this change happened?'

'Goodness.' She put her face close to the baby's. 'When did it all happen, pumpkin? Mummy can't remember. I suppose it was when I got married, roughly, and moved out. Seems the appropriate time, really.'

Smellie rose. 'Fine. Thank you, Mrs Sanderson. Sorry to have taken up your time. I'll let myself out.'

There was no need to put anything in the notebook. He drove quickly back to the office and told Sarah Noonan he did not wish to be disturbed and that she was to take all calls.

15

It was early in the evening when Smellie heard the tentative tapping at his office door and stopped pacing.

'Come in!'

Naismith's head appeared. 'Sorry. Just wondered if you were all right.'

'Fine. No, I'm not. Come in. What time is it?'

'Just after seven, and you haven't had any coffee since midday and I wasn't sure if you'd had lunch. I thought maybe you'd died or gone anorexic or something.'

'No lunch? Is that what it is? I thought I was dying.'

Naismith peered at the sheets of paper covered with scribbled notes and drawings and flowcharts.

'What are you up to?'

'Thinking. Trying to work out the logistics of killing three different women in two different towns on three different dates without being caught. Do you realize how difficult that is, Jimmy? Always assuming our murderer didn't want to be caught, and there's no evidence of a kamikaze attitude. It's bloody difficult, especially if you're driving a distinctive vehicle like a Land Rover van.'

'So?'

'There's no "so" yet. All I've achieved so far is a different way of looking at things. And I think I'm on to something.'

'Can I help?'

'You can take me somewhere I'll be able to refuel the machine. A curry seems the obvious answer.'

'It always is.'

'Am I bad company tonight, Jimmy?'

'Yes. I'm not used to you eating without talking, It's like watching garbage disposal.'

'It's vague, so far. It all seems so unlikely. How easy is it to get new number plates for a vehicle?'

'You go down to Halfords and tell the man the number you want and he asks you what style and says it'll take ten minutes. Then he does you a new plate. Costs about thirteen quid.'

'It's that easy?'

'Yes. I had one done after I hit a pheasant.'

'What about paperwork? Checks on legitimate ownership and so on?'

'I remember the bloke wrote down the number on a form, but that was it. I didn't have to display my registration document or anything, and he didn't ask for my name and address.'

Smellie polished the bowl with the last of the naan bread and popped it into his mouth.

'That must make it pretty easy for your average car thief wanting to change the plates.'

'You said it.'

Smellie sat back and wiped his mouth with the paper napkin. Naismith waited, recognizing a man deep in thought who should not be interrupted.

'Where do you get your anoraks, Jimmy?'

'Lambert's Farm Supplies, out at the auction mart.'

'Good.'

Naismith stared at his friend's face, puzzled. It was frequently difficult to follow Bill Smellie's train of thought.

'Anything you want me to do, Bill?'

'Can't think of anything. I've already put in a request to the Police National Computer; if that doesn't cough up anything then I may have to accept that I'm off on a bum steer.' Smellie drank the last of his lager. 'I'd like coffee.'

They walked back to Divisional HQ, trailing clouds of condensing breath. The pavement was slippery with ice.

'One thing you could do, Jimmy, or get someone to do for you: run a check on all the small industrial units in the town and all the lockup garages. Find out who rented a unit or a garage in the past three or four months. I think I'm looking for someone renting a unit or a garage by phone or letter, maybe paying in cash.'

'OK. You keep giving me these jobs when the people I'll want to talk to are away for the weekend.'

'I don't think we have a time problem. Monday will do. But first thing on Monday.'

They walked into the car-park and stopped beside the Mazda. Smellie shivered.

'Adam Senior will probably be released tomorrow. Fowler and Larch aren't getting anywhere with him.'

'I heard,' Naismith said. 'He won't be dangerous. He won't be able to move without a car up his backside.'

'You were at the inquest this morning. How'd it go?'

'Routine. No problems. But time-consuming, and I'm stacked up with cases.'

'Stay with it, Jimmy. Deal with everything you can, make all the decisions you want; no need to check with me. I need time to think.'

'OK, Bill. Now get off home and get some sleep. You look shagged out.'

'I think that's how I always look nowadays.'

*

Whisky on top of lager. Not a good mixture.

Smellie stood in front of the gas fire in the sitting-room of his flat, waiting for it to warm up. There was dust on the mantelpiece again. Where the hell did it come from?

I want to kill three women. I don't want to be caught. How do I do it?

There was the smell of overheated corduroy from his trousers and he started pacing between the kitchen door and the big window, glass in one hand, the other in his pocket. Away from the fire the room was still cold. He ran his tongue over his lips and tasted the curry sauce.

Motive, means, opportunity.

He was pretty sure about the motive. Not certain, yet, but what he had learned justified some serious consideration. It was the means and opportunity that were difficult.

When the phone rang he was refilling his glass for the third time.

'Are we spending quality time together this weekend, lover?'

'I hope so. I want to buy an anorak.'

'That's not exactly my idea of quality time.'

'You'll be seen in public with me wearing it. I thought you should have some input.'

'Good point.'

'I need a warm jacket for standing around on frozen moors in the middle of the night. I know where Jimmy gets his.'

'Oxfam?'

'That's unfair.'

'Are you coming over now?'

'I'm thinking.'

'Couldn't you think and bonk at the same time?'

'Would you like that?'

'No. You think, I'll read my book.'

'I'll pick you up at half past ten and we'll do some shopping then we'll have lunch.'

'It has to be my treat by now.'

'It is. By a mile.'

When the phone rang he groped but couldn't find it without opening his eyes, which took a serious effort.

'Smellie.'

'You said half past ten. It's now almost eleven.'

'Sorry. Half an hour. Do you want to walk over?'

Jane Grey was reading his *Telegraph* when he appeared in the sitting-room, his hair still wet and uncombed. 'Sorry.'

'When did you go to bed?'

'About six. Not completely sober. You'd better drive.'

'What was your think about? Those women who were murdered?'

Smellie nodded and spent a full five seconds finding his parting and combing his hair.

'I've been trying to work out the logistics of murdering three women over a period of time in three different places without being caught. It's surprisingly difficult. All sorts of dangers.' He pulled on his jacket. 'I'm ready.'

'What about breakfast?'

'I'm saving myself for this monumental lunch you're going to pay for. Wine included, of course.'

'Lambert's Farm Supplies,' Smellie said. 'There it is.'

Jane drove into a large parking area and stopped. 'I've never been here before,' she said. 'I'd no idea. It's a whole new world. What's that over there?'

'The livestock auction mart. That big building is full of cattle pens and pig pens and so on. You should come here on a

Thursday: hundreds of brown men in cloth caps and large boots smelling of dung. The men, not the boots. Land Rovers everywhere.'

Jane opened the door and got out then paused and looked back into the car.

'Coming? Bill? Hey!'

He looked blankly at her then got out of the car and followed her into the building. Jane looked around and grinned.

'Well, it looks as if you can buy sheep dip and milking parlour disinfectant and things for castrating bullocks and wellies and things I do not recognize, but there's also a wide selection of warm jackets.'

He showed no sign of having heard her.

'Bill?'

His brown eyes suddenly focused on hers and he smiled. 'Hi. Let's look for some jackets.'

'You're not with me,' Jane Grey said. 'It's a bit disconcerting, especially when I'm paying. You're not taking full advantage of me.'

'Sorry. Train of thought. Things keep occurring to me. What shall we have?'

'We've already ordered. I'm having the chicken and you're having the lamb. There is wine in your glass.'

'Best place for it. No, the best place is in me. Cheers. You're looking particularly toothsome this evening.'

'It's just after one o'clock in the afternoon.'

'Let's make love.'

'Before or after the main course?'

'Don't exaggerate. When we get back.'

'All right.'

'I love it when you play hard to get.'

Jane shook her head sadly. 'If our relationship lasts another week I'll qualify for an award in the New Year Honours List. Jane Grey, CBE, for services to an idiot policeman. Have you found your murderer?'

'No. But I think I've found the how; from that I should be able to work out the who.'

'So that's it?'

'There's the small matter of proof. And the small matter of possibly being totally wrong. I'll pop back to the office for an hour or so later in the day to set some things in motion then I'm all yours. What's for breakfast?'

It was almost ten o'clock on the Sunday morning when Smellie reached his office, the taste of Jane's full English breakfast still in his mouth. There were six pages of printout from the Police National Computer waiting for him. He studied the information then buzzed through to the big room. Winston answered.

'Come through, please.'

The saturnine DC Winston entered and was waved to a seat. Smellie pushed the sheets of printout across the desk.

'I'm working on the assumption that one of these names is false. A simple phone call should eliminate most of them. Go for it.'

'Yes, sir.'

'Who else is on duty?'

'Sly, sir.'

'Send him in.'

'Are we getting somewhere, sir?'

'Either that or I'm about to waste a whole lot of the taxpayers' money.'

DC Sly lumbered into Smellie's office with a black eye and four stitches across the bridge of his nose.

'Did you win?'

'Yes, sir, thirty-eight–fourteen. I scored a try.'

'Well done. How's the other guy?'

'Carried off, sir, out cold, but we had a pint later. He's all right.'

Smellie nodded. 'Good. I want you to get down to Halfords at the trading estate; they're open on a Sunday.' He scribbled on a piece of paper and passed it to Sly. 'I want to know if someone ordered new vehicle number plates for that number in the past three or four months. If so, I want a description of the individual and any other information you can get. A name and address would be magic. Who else is in the office?'

'No one just at the moment, sir. But DC Lavery could be here in a matter of minutes. She's not doing much.' Sly and Lavery had given up pretending they were just good colleagues.

'Call her.'

Smellie was savouring a cup of fresh coffee in the big room when DC Lavery arrived, slightly out of breath, looking good in tan jeans and a ski jacket, her long blonde hair held back in a scrunchy.

'Morning, sir.'

'Morning, Lavery. You're pretty good at working the computers, aren't you?'

'Yes, sir.'

'Right. There's already a mass of information in the network about blue polypropylene rope. Start searching. I want to know about anyone who bought just three metres of rope in the past six months. To be safe, you'd better also look for four metres. I anticipate that the person we're looking for paid cash, and it's possible there may be a simultaneous purchase of pot plants or bulbs or something like that. If you need help, just shout.'

Naismith called in half an hour later. 'Grossmith and I are at the county council offices. I have a couple of the estates department staff here, looking pretty pissed off, this being Sunday, and there are a couple more at the council head offices in Brickhill.

They've come up with the names and addresses of twenty-nine people or companies who rented garages or industrial units in the county in the past four months. Four of them are in Garrmouth.'

'Good. We'll start with the Garrmouth ones. Do you have a note of how the rent was paid and how the lease was arranged?'

'I'll bring the files.'

It took just a few phone calls to reduce the list of four names to one name.

'J.C. Partick Electronics used an accommodation address in Brickhill, sir,' Naismith said.

Grossmith was operating Smellie's PC. 'And the company name doesn't appear in any directory we have, sir.'

Naismith opened a thin file with the council's logo on the front. 'There's not much here. Copy letter from the estates department to that address referring to Mr Partick's telephone call and confirming that the unit he referred to is vacant and available. A rent is quoted and a lease document enclosed for consideration. Miss Scarth would be happy to meet him and show him the unit, but he seems to have just signed the lease and returned it with a cheque, which is acknowledged and an entry date confirmed. Monday August sixteenth. Mr Partick asked for the key to be posted to him because he would be in Germany and Sweden and was unsure of when he would be back.'

'Let me see,' Smellie said. He studied the letterheads. 'Looks very official, but you can do this on a computer these days. The signature is just a squiggle. How long is the lease for?' He frowned at the document. 'Why do they make these things so complicated? Here we are: for one year, rent payable monthly, either party required to give one month notice of termination. We'll need a history of the payments. Arrange that, Grossmith, then return the other files to the council with my thanks, then copy everything here and send the original file to the lab to see if they can pick up some prints. Then ask HQ to check out the accommodation address in the hope that they can make a connection.'

Naismith waited until Grossmith had gone then looked at Smellie. 'I'm getting lost, Bill. Are we still working on the Blue Rope Strangler?'

'Yes. Get the keys and we'll have a look at this unit.'

16

Smellie drove. The industrial estate was at the far side of the out-of-town shopping complex at the north end, hard by the railway. They studied a schematic layout on a board at the entrance then drove down the spine road past the rows of buildings.

'There,' Naismith said, pointing. 'Right-hand side. That lot.'

Unit 7e was exactly the same as all the others; no window, a rooflight, an aluminium up-and-over door, peeling paintwork and the stains of a leaking gutter on the brickwork. There was no sign of life anywhere in the windswept area.

'Open it, Jimmy.'

Naismith studied the lock, then began to flick through the hundred or so keys on the key ring. Two minutes later the big door screeched open.

'What did you hope to find, Bill?'

There was a small brick construction at the far corner, no doubt an office and toilet, but the rest of the unit was an empty open space with a concrete floor, capable of holding two vehicles end on end.

'Being an optimist, I'd hoped for more than this. Get Scene of Crime here. We'll stay out for the time being.'

*

They sat in the car waiting for Scene of Crime to arrive.

'Are you going to clue me in, Bill?' Naismith asked.

Smellie opened the glove compartment and found a tin of boiled sweets and they both took one.

'I'll wait until I hear what Scene of Crime have to say,' Smellie said. 'This may just be smuggling or tax evasion, but if I'm right then we're on to something interesting. I need you ignorant so I can bounce ideas off you.'

'OK,' Naismith said, unworried. His mobile rang and he answered.

'Winston for you.'

'Thanks.' Smellie took the phone. 'Smellie.'

'You asked me to check on Land Rover vans changing hands in the past four months in the county and surrounding areas, sir. I have a list.'

'Does the name J.C. Partick appear?'

'Hold on, sir.' There was a long silence. 'Yes, sir! A Land Rover van purchased in Doncaster on the twenty-second of August.'

'What day of the week is that?'

'A Sunday, sir.'

'Call them. Ask for a description of the buyer.'

'It was a long time ago, sir.'

'Try. Details on my desk for when I get back, please. Well done, Winston.'

It was the middle of the afternoon and despite Smellie's new down-filled duvet jacket and Naismith's anorak they were both chilled to the bone before Sergeant Mary Goodison could present her preliminary report. Smellie had arranged the delivery of sandwiches and coffee and he and Naismith joined the white-coveralled figures at the back door of the van.

'Well, Sergeant?'

'The floor of the unit has been carefully swept, sir, but we managed to illuminate the tyre marks. Same brand of tyre as on Adam Senior's Land Rover – Avon Ranger Mark II. The results will have to go to the lab before we'll know if it's exactly the same tyres, but in this sort of situation it's not always possible to be sure. Old tyres are better than new tyres: more distinctive damage to the tracks. Adam Senior's tyres were all replaced a few months ago and the tyres here were almost brand new. It looks as if the vehicle was driven in and out just seven or eight times.'

'Anything else?'

'It's not a good locus for prints, sir, but we got some. Again, the fingerprint unit will have to run them through the computer. We also picked up quite a lot of footprints. The ones on top are a man's, size nine, but there's something odd – the prints are blurred, as if the shoes were covered with something. Paper overshoes or socks or poly bags, maybe.'

'And nine is the commonest size.'

'Yes, sir. It's the sort of evidence the defence could pick holes in.'

'Anything in the office or the toilet?'

'A lot of stuff, sir, but it's pretty old and I doubt if it's relevant. It'll go to the lab. I can't give you anything useful at this time.'

It was growing dark when Smellie and Naismith returned to Divisional HQ. They went up to Smellie's office and he read the sheet of paper Winston had left on his desk.

'Green Land Rover van, registration number given, first registered April 1985. Petrol, long wheelbase. Three previous owners. Purchased by J.C. Partick, two thousand two hundred and fifty pounds paid by cheque which was duly honoured. Barclay's Bank. Jimmy, get someone to investigate J.C Partick's banking history. And find out if it would be possible to travel from here to Doncaster conveniently by public transport on a Sunday in order to buy a Land Rover and drive it back the same day.'

The phone rang. It was DC Sly. 'DC Lavery's with me, sir. We both have information for you.'

'Come on in. Bring coffee for Superintendent Naismith and myself. Any doughnuts?'

'Sorry, sir. I ate them.'

'Greedy sod. Get in here.'

They were a good-looking couple, Smellie thought, watching them settle themselves at the other side of the desk. They would probably have children who would grow up to be police officers, Or perhaps giants.

'What do you have, Lavery?'

'HQ had done most of the groundwork on the blue rope, sir. It was just a matter of identifying the three and four metre lengths you mentioned. Four relevant purchases in the past four months in the county. Just one of them also included the purchase of plants. Three metres of blue polypropylene rope.'

She placed a sheet of paper on the desk. Smellie examined it.

'Cash sale. August twenty-ninth. At the DIY supermarket in Brickhill.'

'That's a Sunday, sir.'

'Follow this up. I don't expect the checkout assistant to remember what the purchaser looked like, but try anyway. And find out who supplied the plants to the supermarket.'

'Yes, sir.'

'Sly? I sent you to Halfords.'

'Yes, sir. I drew a blank in Garrmouth but then I called their store in Brickhill and got lucky. We've compared results, sir. The same day someone bought blue rope and plants from the DIY supermarket, someone went into Halfords and paid cash for front and rear plates showing the same registration number as

Adam. Senior's Land Rover. Halfords is just along from the DIY place, and the sales are timed just three-quarters of an hour apart.'

'Name and address? Description?'

'No joy, sir.'

'Well done, both of you.' Smellie leaned back in his chair and swivelled in a circle and braked to a stop. 'Well done.'

'Where are we, sir?' Sly asked.

Smellie grinned at them. 'We're a lot nearer the truth, that's where we are. But still a long way short. There are still things I need to know. Inspector Naismith will have a few of you out at the industrial estate in the morning, talking to people. Anything you can get on the guy who rented Unit 7e. Description, another vehicle, times, dates, the usual. Thanks, everyone. Off you go.'

When the room was empty he called Jane Grey. 'I could be there for Sunday dinner if you pleaded with me hard enough.'

'It's in the oven, The batter's mixed and the potatoes peeled.'

'You're a great little pleader. Is there time to roast the potatoes?'

'I can do anything, Flatfoot.'

Jane woke in the small hours. 'Can't you lie still?'

'Sorry. The brain's going round in circles.'

'So are you, Grunting and sighing, all knees and elbows. Want a cup of chocolate?'

'Let's do that.'

They sat on the couch in the living-room and sipped from the mugs. 'What's your mighty intellect working on?' Jane asked. 'The Blue Rope Strangler?'

'Yes.'

'I saw Adam Senior on the local news, leaving HQ with his solicitor. A short, dignified statement making it clear the police had some grounds for suspicion but that the matter had been cleared up and Mr Senior had been released without a stain on his character. With an official apology.'

'That's not exactly how Fowler and Larch see it. They just haven't been able to pin anything on him.'

'So what are you doing?'

'Trying to look at things from a different angle.'

'You're good at that. It's how you keep getting the answers in my crossword when I'm baffled.'

She finished her chocolate and put the cup on the coffee table and looked at Smellie.

'Oh, for heaven's sake! Don't fall asleep now!'

Naismith knocked and entered Smellie's office to find the big man with his feet up on his desk and a look of concentration on his face.

'Morning, Bill.'

'Morning, Jimmy. Have we a spare body?'

'I can divert people. We're in control again. I've sent four of the squad out to the industrial estate. What do you want doing?'

'I need to find that second Land Rover. If it was sold, then it would be sold under its original registration number, so get someone to check the legitimate sources first. The sale must have happened between the third murder and now.'

'Right. There's a small queue of people waiting to speak to you.'

'Bring them in. Stay and listen.'

Grossmith reported first. 'The council's finance department say the rent for Unit 7e has been paid on time for the past four months.'

Lavery was next. 'Various people supply the DIY supermarket with plants, sir. Including Adam Senior. I have a full list here. They weren't so helpful with the idea of a checkout assistant remembering a cash sale last August. In fact, they found that quite amusing.'

'That's fair enough, I suppose.'

'They have in-store CCTV, sir, but the tapes are reused after a day or two.'

'Thank you, Lavery. Sly?'

'I got HQ to check that accommodation address, sir. The mail addressed to J.C. Partick was collected, not sent on. They've no record of any mail since August. The bill for the service was paid in cash and the arrangement terminated at the end of September. No one remembers what J.C. Partick looked like.'

'Too much to hope for,' Smellie said, 'but I wish, just once, someone would use his eyes and his memory. It would make life so much easier for a hardworking policeman. What about J.C. Partick's banking history?'

'Anstruther's on that now, sir,' Naismith said.

Anstruther appeared half an hour later and read from a fax.

'J.C. Partick opened a business account with Barclay's in Brickhill in early August, sir, with a deposit of three thousand in cash. A second deposit of nine hundred and fifty pounds paid in last Friday. A payment of two thousand two hundred and fifty pounds to a Land Rover agency in Doncaster, a payment of two hundred and forty pounds to Kwik-Fit, four payments to the council, two purchases of petrol, both in Brickhill, then a lot of withdrawals from ATMs here and in Brickhill recently, leaving just loose change in the account.'

'We'll need a sample of his signature. And I want to know if that nine hundred and fifty came from the sale of a Land Rover. And get Kwik-Fit to give you the make and size of the tyres. Chase it up, quick as you can.'

'Smellie? Fowler.'

'Good morning, sir.'

'You'll know we had to let Adam Senior go. I'm still suspicious, but we didn't have enough hard evidence to pin him down. But that's not the end of it: I've put everyone available on the investigation. We're going back over every scrap of evidence, every statement, every interview. Get your people on the ground, Smellie; find something. Extend your house-to-house as far as you want and bugger the expense. Leave Senior's home ground to Robbie Larch, just concentrate on Garrmouth. Talk to everyone who was even remotely connected to Sandra Sim and Laura Beale. If one of them so much as bought her fags from someone with a record I want to know about it. Saturation, concentration, elimination. If you can nail Adam Senior, Smellie, you'll be chief constable by the time you're forty. But don't be blind to the fact that it was maybe someone else.'

'Right, sir,' Smellie said gravely and replaced the phone. It was amazing how Fowler's obsession with the budget seemed to have gone out the window.

He spun in his chair and stared out at small snowflakes drifting out of a charcoal sky then rose and went through to the big room. Winston caught his attention.

'You can get from here to Doncaster by public transport relatively easily, sir, if you're patient and carry your own sandwiches.'

'Thanks.' Smellie sat beside Anstruther. 'Anything on the money which may be from the sale of a Land Rover van?'

'Just came through, sir.'

'A garage in Wimbledon?'

Anstruther shook his head. 'London, but not Wimbledon, sir. Lambeth. They still have it, which is why it wasn't showing up as a recent sale.'

'I want that vehicle impounded and brought back here for forensic examination. Call an Inspector Gorman at the Met, quote my name, arrange it. Tell him it's urgent. If anyone gets sticky, let me know.'

He crossed the room and sat beside Sarah Noonan. 'Sarah, I

need a copy of the *Gazette* covering the wedding of Carol Beale to Keith Sanderson, earlier this year.'

Sarah was married to Jerry Noonan, editor of the *Garrmouth Gazette*.

'No problem. Do you want the glossy?'

Smellie hesitated. 'Why not? And anything else Jerry thinks is relevant.'

'He'll want something exclusive in return.'

'He can have it. That's a promise. The whole story.'

'Sir!' Anstruther caught Smellie's attention. 'The tyres. Kwik-Fit say they were Avon Ranger Mark IIs.'

'Log that. Thank you.'

'There's an air of excitement about you, Bill,' Sarah said. 'Like you've made a breakthrough. Found your strangler?'

'I think I know the motive, Sarah, and I think I know the means, and I can work out the opportunity. I'm just not sure yet whodunit, although it's a very small field. A few searching questions should do the trick.'

'Professor Shane was on for you a few minutes ago.'

'Has she come up with something good?'

'It wasn't business, Bill. She left her home phone number.'

Their eyes met. They knew each other very well.

'If you want,' Sarah said, 'I could call her back and say you're in a very happy relationship at the moment.'

Smellie touched her hand lightly. 'Thanks, love. Tactfully, of course. I don't want to break her heart.'

17

The thin fall of snow in the car-park was spoiled by tyre marks and footprints. Naismith switched on the blower and the wipers to clear the screen.

'Where are we going?'

'It's time we had a word with Adam Senior,' Smellie said.

'We're sure of a big welcome there. Shouldn't you clear this with Fowler first?'

'Definitely.'

'But you're not going to.'

'Slipped my mind.'

There was an unmarked car parked across the road from Adam Senior's nursery, two dark figures inside. Naismith reacted to Smellie's authoritative finger and drove up the short access and braked to a halt in the yard and they climbed out of the car. Adam Senior opened the door of one of the greenhouses and stared at them with an expression of distaste.

'Piss off!'

'Two minutes, sir,' Smellie said peaceably. 'We're still trying to find the person who killed those three women. I'm hoping you may be able to help us identify him. If we don't find the killer, another woman may be murdered.'

'Why should I do anything to help?' It was obvious that Adam

Senior had been nursing his wrath and rehearsing his words and waiting for a chance to express himself. 'I mean, really, you people have tried to torture a confession out of me and failed. Why should I do anything to help you? Why should I give a monkey's toss about you bastards getting an arrest? Why should I give a damn about your careers?'

'Two minutes, sir. Maybe less. Could you look at this, please.'

Smellie unfolded the photocopied page from the *Garrmouth Gazette* and held it up. 'Have you seen these photographs before?'

Senior stared at the page of wedding photographs and shrugged. 'I have no interest in who's marrying who. They're all strangers to me.'

'I glanced round your house, Mr Senior, just in the interest of security, that evening when you agreed to go to the station and be interviewed—'

'Bloody hell, that's the euphemism to end all euphemisms!'

'. . . and I think I remember seeing a copy of the *Gazette*.'

'No, you didn't! Not unless it came wrapped round a bit of fish. I read *The Times*.'

'Have you ever seen this photograph?' Smellie held up the paper again and pointed to one of the blocks.

'No.'

Smellie took an 8" x 8" glossy from the brown envelope. 'This is the original. Have a look at it, please.'

'So?'

'Do you recognize that man, sir? His name is Keith Sanderson.'

Senior shook his head impatiently. 'Never seen him before. Not that he looks particularly memorable.'

'What about the girl?'

'Very pretty, I suppose, but a stranger to me.'

'Her name's Carol Beale, sir,' Smellie said, watching Senior's face carefully. 'Her parents are George and Laura Beale, of Park Crescent, Garrmouth. Do you recognize her now?'

Senior looked closely at the print. 'How could I? I remember the Beales, but when I left Garrmouth they'd no children.'

'I thought you might have recognized her, sir. She's very like you. She may be your daughter by Laura Beale.'

'What?' Senior snatched the print from Smellie and stared at it intently, then shook his head slowly from side to side. 'No, I can't accept that. When was she born?'

'A bit less than nine months after your affair with Mrs Beale came to an end.'

Adam Senior found reading-glasses in the pocket of his padded shirt and put them on and stared at the photograph. 'Are you sure of this, Smellie?' There was no aggression now in his voice.

'Shall we go inside, sir? I have some more questions to ask and it's cold out here.'

Senior nodded and led them along the slab path and in at the back door. The small kitchen suddenly seemed crowded.

'I'm not making coffee for you,' he said, as they sat down round the untidy kitchen table. He was still holding the photograph and seemed unable to take his eyes off it.

'I wonder if you realize the significance of this, sir,' Smellie said, tapping the top edge of the glossy.

'So I screwed Laura a long time ago. Big deal. Judging by the way she treated me I probably wasn't the only one.'

Smellie glanced at Naismith to make sure he was taking notes. 'She dumped you.'

'Quite casually,' Senior said. 'She did her arithmetic and figured out she'd be better off with George, the dullest man in the world but the man with the nice house and the new car and the prospects.' His voice dripped scorn. 'Laura chose security. She came from a pathetic little middle-class family, all desperately respectable, virgin on the marriage night, pre-war values, all that crap. I was her little excursion into the real world. But she didn't fancy being tied to an unemployed former Navy officer with no money and a foul little room next door to people who screamed at each other all night so she went back to her husband and kept her mouth shut. I didn't care. I was better off without her.'

'You left your wife and rented a flat expecting Laura Beale to join you and she didn't. You cared. You took the affair very seriously.'

'Who told you that?'

'Anna Anders got it from Laura Beale,' Smellie said. 'Charlie Findlay got it from you. I got it from them. I also spoke to your former wife. She has three grown-up children and runs a pre-school nursery in Liverpool and seems very happy, if that's of any interest to you.'

Senior stubbed out his cigarette in the overflowing ashtray. 'I'm glad about that. Janice and I should never have got married. It was a mistake. The marriage was dead long before I got together with Laura. I'm not sure if that has any significance.'

'It's significant, sir. It's part of the big picture.'

'So?' Senior looked angrily at Smellie. 'Are you really still trying to prove I killed Laura Beale? After twenty-something years? Out of revenge, do you think? It's a pretty shaky motive. If anyone has a motive, it's George Beale.'

'What motive is that, sir?'

'Oh, don't come the vacant PC Plod act with me! You're no country bumpkin, Detective Superintendent Smellie! George caught Laura and me kissing at a party in the Anders' house one night; he was too much of a wet to do anything about it, but he was suspicious. Then, years later, he discovered. . . .'

'Discovered what, sir?'

'That I was the father of his daughter, I suppose. That I'd got his wife pregnant. That he'd been a patsy all these years.'

'How did he find out, sir?'

'I don't know. Maybe Laura just happened to mention it one day when she was feeling particularly spiteful. Maybe George just suddenly spotted the resemblance. Ask him, for heaven's sake! Don't ask me!'

'So you now agree that Carol Sanderson is your daughter?'

Senior stared at Carol Beale's wedding photograph and shrugged. 'You've persuaded me,' he said quietly.

'That was quick.'

'Don't be bloody sarcastic.'

'And? What did George Beale do when he found out Carol wasn't his daughter?'

'Why ask me?' Adam Senior pulled a cigarette from the packet and thumbed his lighter and blew smoke across the table. 'But I wouldn't be surprised if he killed Laura and tried to frame me for it. And bloody nearly succeeded. All the time those bastards Fowler and Larch were doing their hard-man-soft-man act I kept telling them there had to be a second Land Rover, one just like mine, because I wasn't in those places at those times. It never occurred to me it might all be deliberate, that I was being set up, because I'd no idea what the motive was. I just accepted this stupid idea of a religious paranoid killing a particular brand of prostitute and Laura Beale being a mistake, like they said. But Laura was the prime target and the other two women were a blind. Surely that points straight at George Beale.'

'Or perhaps you killed Laura Beale and tried to frame her husband,' Smellie said.

'Are you really as thick as you look, Smellie? He set me up! He killed those women and made it look like I was responsible! The murder of the two prostitutes was just a smokescreen, to make it look like Laura had been strangled by a serial killer, so you guys wouldn't look too closely for a motive going back twenty years.'

'An intriguing theory, sir,' Smellie said. 'We've, found a fake bank account in the name of J.C. Partick Electronics; we've tracked down the purchase of a Land Rover just like yours; we've established that new registration plates showing the number of your Land Rover were bought at Halfords. You haven't had new plates made in the past few months, have you?'

'No. You've seen my van, dammit; the plates are original.'

'I didn't ask if you'd fitted them,' Smellie said. 'We've found evidence that a vehicle with your registration number was fitted with four new tyres, the same brand as you have on your vehicle. But we know you'd already fitted new tyres after receiving a warning some months ago about having insufficient tread, so we're acting on the assumption that the new tyres were fitted to this second vehicle with the intention of implicating you.'

'You're proving my point, Smellie. I was set up. And it had to be by George Beale.'

Smellie sat back and sighed. 'Fine so far, but if George Beale arranged all this – and I say if – then he did a very good job of covering his tracks. We can't find anyone who can say with any certainty that Beale set up the bank account or bought the Land Rover or the tyres. People aren't that observant. And there's the blue rope: there are miles of it in the county and you have some of it. And there are the traces of soil and vegetable matter on Laura Beale's clothes, pointing to your nursery: how did George Beale arrange that? And where did he hide the Land Rover? He couldn't just park it in his garage at home. In other words, it's very easy to substitute you for George Beale.'

'So he rented a garage somewhere, Smellie.' Adam Senior spoke as if to a child. 'I'm sure he could do that by post, without having to meet anyone. Which would require an accommodation address, of course. Have you checked out that possibility?'

'No, sir,' Smellie said. 'We didn't think of that. That's very clever. You're very quick.'

Senior stared at him. 'Why do I get the impression you're playing me like a fish, Smellie?'

'I really don't know, sir.'

'An accommodation address. Follow that up. And all he needed to do to get the appropriate soil and so on all over his wife's clothes would be to buy one of my pot plants or trays of seedlings. They all carry my label. Try the DIY superstores. You might even find a simultaneous purchase of a few metres of blue polypropylene rope.'

Smellie frowned and nodded. 'All this is very interesting, Mr Senior, but I still can't see any evidence which will definitely pin George Beale. It's all very well for you and me to sit here and come up with theories, but I have to prepare a case which will stand up in court, and you've no idea how easy it is to be a bit uncertain about something on the stand and watch a skilled brief take your evidence apart and rubbish it. We have to be absolutely dead certain of everything.'

'Like what?' Senior demanded. 'What more do you need, for heaven's sake?'

'Eye witnesses. Fingerprints. DNA. Hard evidence.'

'Fowler and Larch kept hammering away at evidence on CCTV.'

Smellie nodded. 'A Land Rover van was seen in Shore Road on the night Sandra Sim was murdered, but no registration number was seen. On the night Laura Beale was murdered, a Land Rover van drove past the Asda camera but, again, the number was not seen. Anyway, where is this bloody Land Rover? They must be hard things to hide, but we can't find it.'

'He sold it, you stupid bugger! He put the original plates back on and sold it!'

'What happened to the fake plates?'

Senior raised his hands in a plea for divine understanding. 'He destroyed them! He buried them! He put them out with the rubbish. I don't know. That's your job.'

'That's a good answer, Mr Senior,' Smellie said. 'Now give me a good answer to this question: could you lay hands on three thousand pounds cash? More precisely, could you have laid hands on that sum of money three months ago?'

'Only by selling my business or my house, Mr Smellie. I survive, but success is measured in the size of my overdraft.'

'I'm going to instruct a detailed investigation of your financial affairs. . . .'

'Go right ahead. If you find anyone owing me money, let me know.'

'A business like this,' Smellie said, 'you must do a lot of cash sales. And it would be impossible for the Inland Revenue to keep accurate track of just how many plants and things you produce. You must have a fair old income that doesn't go through the books.'

Senior studied the end of his cigarette. 'It happens. But not three thousand pounds' worth. That's laughable.'

Naismith's mobile sounded; he answered and passed the phone to Smellie. 'Sarah.'

'Yes, Sarah?'

'There's a Land Rover van on its way down from London, Bill. It should arrive late in the afternoon. It will be delivered to the garage at HQ.'

'Speak to Robbie Larch, tell him what's happening. I want it gone over minutely. I especially want the back of the number plates checked for prints.'

Senior looked up from the glossy as Smellie closed the call.

'You've found the second Land Rover?'

'Yes, sir.'

'Where?'

'In London. It was sold to a dealer just last Wednesday.'

'So find out where George Beale was that day.'

'George Beale has been at home since his wife was murdered, sir.'

'Can't have been. And on Wednesday I was still in a small room with two fat pigs trying to force a confession out of me. Work on that, Detective Superintendent Smellie.'

'I shall, sir. Thank you for your time.'

Smellie and Naismith rose. Senior held up the black and white glossy.

'May I keep this? I'll pay for it.'

'With my compliments, sir.'

As Naismith drove out on to the road along the shore a figure stepped smartly out of the parked car and raised a hand and crossed the road.

'Sergeant Greenman, sir. I'm with Mr Larch's squad. It's Mr Smellie, isn't it, sir? And Mr Naismith?'

'That's right, Sergeant,' Smellie said.

'I called in when you arrived, sir. Chief Detective Inspector Fowler is very anxious to know just what the . . . . he'd like to know why you've been talking to Adam Senior, sir, without notifying him first.'

'Pissed off, was he?' Naismith asked.

'Yes, sir. Very.'

'Call him back, Sergeant,' Smellie said. 'Tell him I'm checking on possible new information and that I'll be in touch if I can get confirmation.'

'Yes, sir. Thank you, sir.'

Naismith waited until he had dropped into fifth gear before he spoke.

'Checking on possible new information. Be in touch if you can get confirmation. Bill, that is as vague as anything I've ever heard in my life.'

'I rather liked it myself.'

'Where are we going?'

'Under the circumstances, I think we'd better have a word with George Beale. I didn't want to, just at this time, but I suspect I may have raised a bit of a stink and I might not get the chance if I don't act now. I'm going to have to ask him if he knows Carol isn't really his daughter, and I'm not looking forward to that.'

'Adam Senior seemed to have it all worked out.'

'He's not daft, You need a pretty high IQ to get into the Navy as an officer.'

Naismith accelerated past a tractor and trailer. 'That was a nice touch, him asking if he could keep the photograph of Carol. Touched the heartstrings, that did.'

'You old cynic.'

18

They saw George Beale at the lounge window as they arrived, waiting for them in response to Smellie's call.

'Come in, Mr Smellie. Hello, Mr Naismith. I've started a pot of coffee. Have a seat in the lounge.'

The policemen discarded their anoraks and sat together on the couch. The marmalade cat occupied an armchair, one leg hanging indolently. Maybe I could manage a cat, Smellie thought; Jane could feed it if I were away. It would be pleasant to have a living creature in the flat all the time.

George Beale came through from the kitchen with a tray and placed it carefully on the coffee table. Matching crockery, of course. He left the cafetière to infuse.

'So, Mr Smellie, what's the latest? Any news of when Laura's body will be released for burial? It's all becoming a bit of a strain.'

'I think that will happen very soon, sir.'

Beale sank into an armchair beside the log-effect gas fire. 'I'll be glad when this is all over. So much stress. I really had no idea the Press could be so insensitive; God knows how often they've taken my photograph or phoned me or Carol or Graham or the office.'

Smellie nodded. 'It will end quite suddenly. I have some questions to ask you, sir. They're the kind of questions you may not want to answer, or may want to lie about, but it's important that you answer truthfully. Inspector Naismith will be taking notes.'

'I see.' Beale took the lid off the cafetière and stirred the coffee then slowly depressed the plunger. 'We'll give it a moment to settle. Go on.'

'When did you discover your wife had been intimate with Adam Senior?'

George Beale's right hand jerked involuntarily. His eyes flickered behind the glasses. He ran his palm back over his bare scalp and exhaled shakily.

'What makes you think my wife was unfaithful?'

'I have statements from Margot Arbuthnot, Anna Anders, Charles Findlay and Gordon Liddescroft. It seems it wasn't much of a secret.'

'That bunch of weirdos. Does the whole bloody world know my family secrets?'

'Not the whole world, sir; a handful of people. When did you find out?'

Beale made an effort to compose himself. 'I suspected, long ago, but. . . . I suppose I didn't want to know. Or maybe I knew but couldn't really believe it. I labour under the disadvantage of being naively honest, Mr Smellie. It's very easy to fool me. I trust people when others might have their doubts. I can clearly recall thinking, one night, in the Anders house – OK, so they were kissing, so what, it's a party and we've all been drinking and people do silly things, that's all it is. But you don't forget.'

'This was back in the days when Adam Senior lived in Ismay Place?'

'Yes.'

'Were they aware that you'd seen them?'

'No. At least, I don't think so. Laura didn't say anything.'

'And when did you realize Carol isn't your daughter?'

'What?' Beale glared at Smellie, his face reddening.

'I asked, sir, when you realized Carol isn't your daughter.'

'Isn't she my daughter?'

'No, sir. You knew that. I just wondered when you found out.'

'I don't think I want to go on with this,' Beale said angrily. 'It's not right. You've no right to harass me like this.'

'I phoned Carol just a few minutes ago,' Smellie said. 'I think you remember very well just when you discovered she's Adam Senior's daughter by your wife. It's not the sort of thing you'd forget.'

It was a long time before George Beale spoke. When he did there was a terrible anger in his voice.

'Her wedding day.'

'And what happened on Carol's wedding day?'

There was a tremor in Beale's hand as he poured the coffee.

'What happened was that Carol arrived here to get dressed with her hair cut short. She'd been wearing it right down her back since she was a little girl. Long and straight and shiny black. Suddenly it was short and wavy. I could hardly believe my eyes. It was like meeting someone for the first time.'

'And?'

George Beale sighed. 'And I realized she wasn't my daughter.'

Smellie reached into his pocket and produced the photograph he had borrowed from Anna Anders. It showed Carol Beale in her late teens, half-turned towards her brother, laughing, the black hair spilling down her back to her waist.

'When I saw this photograph I didn't immediately recognize Carol,' Smellie said. 'I'd only ever seen her with short hair. It made me take a second look, and that's when I noticed the similarity between her and Adam Senior. In the eyes, mainly, and the mouth and the build. She doesn't look like you or your wife. Or her brother.'

Beale nodded. 'It was pretty obvious. God knows how I'd

missed it all these years.' He looked towards the lounge door and his eyes went out of focus. 'She walked in that door and did a sort of curtsy and spun round and said something like, "How about this, then".' I think it was her way of saying she was starting a new life, marrying Keith, expecting a baby, growing up, leaving us.'

'What else did you see, sir?'

'I saw Adam Senior. Clear as daylight. In the hair and the eyes and the mouth and the height, everything. Even in the way she walked. And I remembered that night in the Anders' house.'

'How did you react?'

'Badly. I went through the day in a sort of daze. God knows how I managed to do all the things I had to do as father of the bride. I drank far more than I usually do but it didn't seem to have any effect. I waited until that evening, after the reception, after Laura and I were back here alone. She knew. She'd known all day what was wrong. We sat down, right here, and I just looked at her and she burst into tears and said she was sorry and pleaded with me not to stop loving Carol. She said all the blame was hers, not Carol's. You try not to have favourites among your children, Mr Smellie, but you do, and Carol was my favourite. Graham was always Laura's favourite. It was accepted in the family. But discovering that your delightful daughter is the child of another man is a rather severe test of your love. Carol doesn't know about all this, of course, and I don't want her ever to know, but she's aware that my feelings towards her have changed. I haven't been able to hide my feelings completely. And there's Marie, the baby, my first grandchild. She's not related to me in any way, but. . . .'

He closed his eyes and removed his glasses and covered his face with his hand. When he spoke his voice was a shaky whisper.

'You can't not love a baby. It's impossible. A baby is so innocent of everything. And Carol spent more than twenty years with us, in this house, being my daughter. I rationalized the situation by persuading myself that if she'd been adopted I'd have had no problems about accepting her and loving her.'

'How did you feel about your wife?'

Beale shook out a neatly folded handkerchief and wiped his eyes and blew his nose.

'Excuse me.' He took a deep breath and exhaled. 'When you've been married for twenty-five years a lot of the communication between you doesn't need words. I could see Laura regretted what she'd done, and I could see she knew I was deeply hurt and it was breaking her up. We didn't say much to each other for a couple of days. For a week, really.'

He stopped. Smellie kept silent, waiting. George Beale had more to say.

'After all that time you don't want it to end, Mr Smellie. You're half of something, half of a partnership; you don't want to be alone. All your adult life your decisions and efforts and everything have been for the two of you and the children. There's not much passion left, just . . . sharing. Being friends. Being together. And you find yourself thinking that your own male vanity is of no importance when compared with being able to guarantee your children and your grandchild a solid family home to come back to. Time passes; you adjust. You realize you're too old and tired to make some silly gesture like breaking up and going off to live on your own somewhere. You're certainly not interested in starting some new relationship with a stranger. So you go on from day to day and gradually the hurt doesn't hurt so much. And it was all a long time ago.'

Smellie drank the last of his coffee. It was good and there was more in the cafetière but it hardly seemed the right moment to ask for a refill.

'How did you and Adam Senior get on, back in the days when he lived in Ismay Place, Mr Beale?'

George Beale shrugged. 'We didn't like each other, much. It wasn't anything serious, more a matter of two men not being on the same wavelength. I tried, but we never clicked. As it happens, I don't think he formed a close friendship with anyone else, unless maybe Charlle Findlay. They'd been in the Navy together.'

'Do you think Senior knew Carol was his daughter?'

'Laura told me he didn't know.'

Smellie leant forward on the couch. 'When did she say that, sir?'

'That night, after the wedding. She didn't think Senior ever knew she was pregnant. She didn't know herself until after they'd broken up. As far as I can make out, Senior left his wife expecting Laura to follow him, but she didn't. It was only then she discovered she was pregnant.'

'And she chose to stay with you, sir.'

'So it seems.'

'She admitted all this to you?'

'In bits and pieces. We had a long night of revelations and tears and apologies and anger. I was angry, not her. She reassured me that Graham was my son. She made the point that I loved Carol even though she wasn't my daughter and pleaded with me not to change that. I'm sorry. Excuse me.'

He rose abruptly and went through to the kitchen. Naismith looked to Smellie and received a cautioning hand. They heard the sound of a tap running then Beale returned and sat down, his face shiny.

'What were your feelings about Adam Senior, Mr Beale?' Smellie asked. 'That night, I mean, when you found out.'

'If he'd come to the door that evening I would have tried to kill him with my bare hands. I don't lose my temper much, never did, but that night would have been different. God knows how effective I'd have been. I'm not exactly Action Man.'

'Does the name J.C. Partick mean anything to you, Mr Beale?' Smellie asked.

'No.'

'Unit 7e at the industrial estate at the north end?'

'No.'

'You went up to London just after your wife was murdered, to break the news to her mother. What day was that?'

'Wednesday, I think.'

'How did you travel?'

'By train. I never take the car to London.'

'How did you pay for your ticket?'

'Cash. What. . . ?'

'Meet anyone you know on the train, anyone who could confirm your story?'

'I don't remember anyone. Why should I need to have my story confirmed?'

'Do you still have the tickets?'

'I shouldn't think so, no.'

'It would help if you did, sir.'

Beale displayed signs of impatience. 'Mr Smellie, what's all this about? Why all these questions? I'm very careful about holding on to any paperwork that matters, but I get rid of all the bumph that clutters up our lives nowadays. I don't keep old rail tickets. Why should I have to prove I went to London to visit Gran? I did. Ask her.'

'I'm sure you did, sir. It's how you travelled that interests me. I think you drove to London in a Land Rover van which you then sold to a dealer in Lambeth for nine hundred and fifty pounds. Which was way below the two thousand two hundred and fifty you paid for it in Doncaster but, of course, you were desperate to get rid of it. It's the sort of transaction a sales assistant would remember. I'll be having that checked out; I expect to learn that the sales assistant remembers you as mug of the month. And we'll be checking the paperwork for your fingerprints, of course. And the lease document for Unit 7e.'

George Beale stared at Smellie, then at Naismith, then at Naismith's notebook then back to Smellie.

'I can't believe this. You think I killed Laura. And those other two women?'

'Yes, sir. It's not just a matter of thinking it: I know it. I've known it since last Saturday, when I went to buy a jacket from a firm next door to the auction mart and saw four Land Rovers parked in a line, all looking just like each other. That's when I saw how easy it would be to lay a false trail by buying a vehicle like Adam Senior's Land Rover van and fitting it with number plates and tyres to match his. All you had to do was to set up Adam Senior as a loony serial killer who killed two prostitutes and then your wife by mistake. The letter to Robbie Larch was very effective. A touch of genius, really.'

George Beale deliberately picked up his cup and sipped the coffee and replaced the cup in the saucer.

'I won't protest my innocence, Mr Smellie. This is all too fanciful for a reasoned reply. I'll just ask what actual proof you have, what definite, incontrovertible, rock-solid evidence you could present in court.'

'The Land Rover is in the police garage right now, Mr Beale, with the experts going over it with the most amazing selection of modern scientific techniques. They'll look very carefully at the petrol cap and the underside of the door handles. That's the sort of place a man might forget he's left his fingerprints. And on the bonnet stay and the hand brake lever and the wiper control.'

George Beale was shaking his head slowly from side to side. 'You won't find my prints on that vehicle, Mr Smellie. Until right now I didn't even know it existed.'

'And the back of the original number plates, of course.'

Both Smellie and Naismith were watching George Beale's face

intently. They both caught the tiny flicker of doubt in his eyes. He clasped his hands together and touched his fingertips to his lower lip and frowned.

'No. No, I don't think you'll find anything there.'

'You sound uncertain, sir. Are you feeling unwell? You've gone quite pale. It was all very carefully planned, but did you make a mistake with the original number plates? Did you remove them when you weren't wearing gloves, intending to wipe them before you replaced them? I suppose the self-tapping screws were rusted in and you had trouble with them and maybe had to take your gloves off. Is that how it was? Would you like a glass of water, sir? Should I call a doctor? You don't look at all well. And you wore something over your shoes when you were in Unit 7e, to disguise your footprints. And you rented the unit without meeting anyone from the council. You bought everything you needed by cash – the rope, the soil, the number plates. You made sure the Land Rover was seen and you left a tyre print up on the moor. The one thing that went wrong was that the number plate wasn't seen clearly on the Asda CCTV. You strangled Karen Potter and Sandra Sim and your wife and left a trail pointing directly to Adam Senior, knowing we'd find out about his liaison with your wife. Then you waited for him to be punished for what he did to you twenty-odd years ago. I think you're basically a good-natured man, Mr Beale, a tolerant man, an honest man, but you couldn't forgive your wife and Adam Senior for creating the daughter you've loved for twenty years. You couldn't forgive them for the fact that Marie, your granddaughter, is in no way related to you. You had a powerful motive.'

'So did Adam Senior,' Beale whispered. 'His daughter lived with me all her life. He was denied the delight of having a child.'

'He didn't know,' Smellie said. 'Until today he didn't know he had a daughter. The news floored him. He couldn't take his eyes off the photograph. Maybe now he has a motive for murder; maybe now he hates your wife enough to kill her, because she never told him and he missed out on all that. But she's already dead. Are you feeling all right, sir? You look very bad. You've gone white.'

Naismith stopped writing in his notebook and looked up. George Beale detected the motion and raised his head.

'I'm so tired,' he said quietly. 'This has all been a terrible strain. I've been waiting for this moment.'

'Go on, sir, Get it off your chest.'

'I regret killing those two prostitutes. Laura had to die, of course, for what she did. It was immensely satisfying, killing her, telling her why. I just hope she heard me while she was struggling. But I regret the other two women. They seemed perfectly nice young women, despite what they did for a living. They weren't guilty of anything that justified what I did to them. They were just . . . part of the plot. Their job was to make Laura's murder look like a mistake.'

He looked to Smellie.

'Do you think Adam Senior will try to get in touch with Carol? I couldn't bear that.'

'He's her father, sir. He has that right. I wouldn't be surprised if Carol got in touch with him, or he got in touch with her. I can't help thinking they might become friends.'

George Beale seemed unconscious of the tears running down his cheeks.

'Marie needs a grandfather to spoil her. All babies do. I just wish I could be sure Adam Senior is the right man. Keep an eye on them, Mr Smellie. Please accept that responsibility.'

It was late in the evening before everything that had to be done had been done and Smellie had spent half an hour with the furious Chief Detective Superintendent Fowler. Naismith watched the rotund figure storm out of Smellie's office and vanish down the stairs and picked up the phone and tapped out a number.

When he entered Smellie's office ten minutes later the big man was sitting in his swivel chair with his feet up on the window ledge, looking out at the night. Naismith opened the bottom drawer of the desk and found two glasses and took the half bottle of Bell's from his pocket and poured two large ones.

'Rough, Bill?'

'Not really, Jimmy. You know me. When I'm in the right I can be incredibly good-natured, which must be infuriating for your average senior officer who has been trying to convict the wrong fella. Cheers.'

'Cheers.' Naismith moved a chair and sat down and put his feet on the windowsill next to his friend's. 'Snowing again.'

'It won't lie. You may smoke.'

'Thanks.' There was a pause while Naismith lit a cigarette. 'Robbie Larch phoned. George Beale's prints are on the back of the front number plate. Not the rear, oddly enough, but definitely on the front.'

'Good to know.'

'That was clever, telling him he'd gone white, asking him if he wanted a glass of water or a doctor.'

Smellie grinned. 'We had a Latin teacher at school, Killer Kemp, one of the most irritating wanks you can imagine. Every so often, by arrangement, we'd get rid of him for a day or two by saying: "Are you feeling all right, sir? You look very pale, sir. Should we send for Matron, sir? Maybe you should sit down, sir. Would you like a glass of water, sir?" The poor sod would become ill in front of our very eyes and stagger off and Miss MacIntyre would stand in for him and we would spend the Latin periods staring fixedly at her monumental tits. They were bigger than Wales. Applied psychology, Jimmy. Small boys can do it; why not senior investigating officers?'

'It worked,' Naismith said. 'He actually went white.'

'I must try it on Norman Fowler some time.'

'I thought you might be hungry,' Naismith said, 'so I called Jane and suggested she collect Norma and we'll all meet in the Raj in half an hour.'

'My treat.'

'Really? The whole thing? Not just the water?'

'The whole thing.'

'Bloody hell!'